Dead Pigeon

Dead Pigeon
WILLIAM CAMPBELL GAULT

Introduction by Bill Pronzini

Carroll & Graf Publishers, Inc.
New York

First Carroll & Graf edition 1992

Carroll & Graf Publishers, Inc.
260 Fifth Avenue
New York, NY 10001

ISBN: 0-88184-839-5

Manufactured in the United States of America

To Sally Sergenian, ardent reader

SOME WORDS ABOUT WILLIAM CAMPBELL GAULT

By Bill Pronzini

Bill Gault is that rara avis, a legend in his own time.

Few writers have had a career as long, distinguished, honored, and critically acclaimed. He has been a professional writer for more than half a century, having made his first sale in the midst of the Great Depression. His credits include scores of quality novels, both mysteries and juvenile sports fiction, and hundreds of short stories, many of which have been anthologized. Among his awards are an Edgar from the Mystery Writers of America and the Life Achievement Award from the Private Eye Writers of America. Noted author and critic Anthony Boucher said of him: "[He is] a fresh voice—a writer who sounds like nobody else, who has ideas of his own and his own way of uttering them." Another of his peers, Dorothy B. Hughes, in reviewing one of his novels stated that he "writes with passion, beauty, and with an ineffable sadness which has previously been found only in Raymond Chandler."

Born in Milwaukee in 1910, Gault began writing while in high school and continued to write sporadically during a brief stint at the University of Wisconsin and then while holding down a series of odd jobs. But his early efforts displeased him; he made no attempt to market any of his stories until 1936. He was working as a sole cutter in a shoe factory when he entered a story called "Inadequate" in a Milwaukee *Journal*-McClure Newspaper Syndicate short story contest. The judges found it to be anything but inadequate, awarding it the fifty-dollar first prize.

Spurred on by this success, Gault wrote and placed several more stories with the McClure Syndicate, then in 1937 entered the wide-open pulp fiction field with the sale of a drag-racing story, "Hell Driver's Partnership," to *Ace Sports*. Over the next fifteen years he was a prolific provider of tales of mystery, detection, sports, both light and spicy romance, and science fiction to such pulps as *Scarlet Adventuress, 10-Story Detective* (which published his first mystery story, "Crime Collection," in its January 1940 issue), *Detective Fiction Weekly, The Shadow, Clues, All-American Football, Strange Detective Mysteries, Adventure, Dime Mystery, Dime Detective, Doc Savage, Argosy, Detective Tales, Five Novels Monthly,* and *Thrilling Wonder,* and to such "slick" and specialty magazines as *The Saturday Evening Post* (which published three of his sports stories), *Grit, McClure's,* and *Young Catholic Messenger.* In the late forties he was a cover-featured contributor to the most revered of detective magazines, *Black Mask,* in whose pages he published nine stories—five of them featuring an offbeat, Duesenberg-driving private detective named Mortimer Jones.

When the pulp markets collapsed in the early 1950's, their once-lofty eminence having been undermined by paperback original novels and that insidious new medium, television, Gault turned his hand to book-length works. In 1952, he published the first of his thirty-three novels for young adults, *Thunder Road,* which earned him numerous plaudits from readers, reviewers, and educators and which remained in print for more than three decades. That same year saw publication of his first mystery, *Don't Cry for Me,* one of the seminal crime novels of its time.

Prior to *Don't Cry for Me,* the emphasis in mystery fiction was on the mystery itself: whodunit and why. Gault's novel broke new ground in that its whodunit elements are subordinate to the personal and inner lives of its major characters and to a razor-sharp depiction of the socioeconomic aspects of its era—an accepted and widely practiced approach utilized by many of today's best writers of mystery and detective fiction. *Don't Cry for Me*'s narrator, Pete Worden, is anything but a standard hero; he lives a disorganized and unconventional life, walking a thin line between respectability and corruption, searching for purpose and identity. His girlfriend, Ellen, wants him to be one thing; his brother, John, who controls the family purse strings, wants him to be another; and some of his "friends" want him to be a third. What finally puts an end to Worden's aimless lifestyle is the discovery in his apartment of a murdered hoodlum with whom he had a fistfight the previous night. Hounded by both the police and members of the underworld, he is not only forced into his own hunt for the killer but to resolve his personal ambivalence as well. Gault's fellow crime novelist, Fredric Brown, said that the novel "is not only a beautiful chunk of story but, refreshingly, it's about people instead of characters, people so real and vivid that you'll think you know them personally. Even more important, this boy Gault can *write*, never badly and sometimes like an angel." Gault's other peers, the members of the Mystery Writers of America, agreed, voting *Don't Cry for Me* a Best First Novel Edgar.

Gault's subsequent mysteries are likewise novels of character and social commentary, whether they feature average individuals or professional detectives as protagonists. Many have unusual and/or sports backgrounds, in particular his nonseries books. For instance, *The Bloody Bokhara* (1952) deals with the selling of valuable Oriental rugs and carpets in his native Milwaukee; *Blood on the Boards* (1953) has a little-theater setting in the Los Angeles area, where Gault and his family moved in the postwar forties; *The Canvas Coffin* (1953) concerns the fight game and is narrated by a middleweight champion boxer; *Fair Prey* (1956), published under the pseudonym Will Duke, has a golfing background; *Death Out of Focus* (1959) is about Hollywood filmmakers and script writers, told from an "insider's" point of view.

The bulk of Gault's thirty-one crime novels—as well as many of his short stories—showcase series detectives. One of his first was Mortimer Jones, in the pages of *Black Mask;* another pulp detective hero, Honolulu private eye Sandy McKane, debuted in *Thrilling Detective* in 1947 and solved a handful of other cases in the Hawaiian Islands (where Gault was stationed with the 166th Infantry during World War II). Italian P.I. Joe Puma, who operates out of Los Angeles, was created for the paperback original market in the fifties, first as the narrator of a pseudonymous novel, *Shakedown* (1953, as by Roney Scott), and then of several books published under Gault's own name between 1958 and 1961, notably *Night Lady* (1958) and *The Hundred-Dollar Girl* (1961). Puma is also the featured performer in more than a dozen excellent novelettes published in the fifties and sixties in such magazines as *Manhunt* and *Ellery Queen's Mystery Magazine.*

But Gault's most enduring and successful fictional creation is Brock "The Rock" Callahan, an ex-L.A. Rams lineman turned private eye, who initially appeared in *Ring Around Rosa* in 1955. Callahan, along with his lady friend, interior decorator Jan Bonnet, did duty in six novels over the next eight years. In a rave review of the best of these, *Day of the Ram* (1956), *The New York Times* called Callahan "surely one of the major private detectives created in American fiction since Chandler's Philip Marlowe."

After the publication of *Dead Hero* in 1963, Gault decided to abandon detective fiction and concentrate on the more lucrative juvenile market. He did not return to a life of fictional crime until nearly twenty years later, when the young-adult vein had been played out; and when he did return, it was exclusively with an older, wiser, and changed

11

Callahan: now married to Jan and, thanks to a substantial inheritance, living in comfortable semiretirement in the California coastal city of San Valdesto (a thinly disguised Santa Barbara, Gault's adopted home for many years). The new series of Callahan books began with *The Bad Samaritan* (1982) and was followed that same year by *The Cana Diversion,* in which Gault also brought back Joe Puma—*dead*. The central premise of *The Cana Diversion* is Puma's murder and Callahan's search for the killer, a surprising tour de force that earned Gault yet another award, the Private Eye Writers of America Shamus for Best Paperback Original of 1982.

Dead Pigeon is the seventh in the new series of Brock Callahan mysteries, and the fourteenth Callahan overall. It is also Bill Gault's sixty-fourth published novel, marking the fortieth anniversary of the novel-writing phase of his career and the fifty-sixth anniversary of his first professional sale. It begins with the mysterious death of Callahan's old college football roommate, then follows a twisty path through a maze peopled by religious cultists, gangsters, cops both honest and crooked, a couple of designing women, and a stockbroker who may or may not be guilty of illegalities. Among its virtues are such vintage Gault stocks-in-trade as finely tuned dialogue, wry humor, sharp social observation, a vivid evocation of both upscale and downscale lifestyles in that world unto itself, southern California. Most importantly, it is about people rather than characters—people, in Fredric Brown's words, so real and vivid that you'll think you know them personally.

More than that no reader can ask of any writer.

And no writer can give more to any reader, especially when he happens to be a living legend at the age of eighty-two.

Dead Pigeon

CHAPTER ONE

It was raining that Tuesday morning when I picked up Heinie at his bar and grill in Beverly Hills. "Rain in May," he said. "How often do we get that?"

"Not often enough," I said.

"The missus come with you?"

I shook my head. "She's on her way to Tacoma for her annual visit to her aunt. I was going with her—until I got your call."

"And she gave you no static?"

"Why should she?"

"Most wives would take a real sour view of their hubbies going to the funeral of a guy they never knew." He shook his head. "And the funeral of a stoolie, yet."

"Not my Jan. She knows why I'm here. The guy saved my life, Heinie."

He smiled. "Owing and being owed, that's your Bible, isn't it?"

"Yours, too, Heinie."

He nodded. "That's why I'm going with you. May as well take Sunset all the way. The mortuary is in Brentwood."

Around the long curves of Sunset Boulevard in the misty rain in silence. I don't know what Heinie was thinking about; I was thinking about Mike Gregory, now deceased. He'd had two years at Stanford as a second-string quarterback, one year with E.F. Hutton as an unsuccessful broker, four years as a used-car salesman, and too many years as a drunkard and informant for yours truly when I was operating in lotus land.

What a waste! A bright guy, Mike Gregory; he could have been a high school or college coach. He could have been the first-string quarterback at Stanford if he had taken the game seriously. Stanford is a school that has graduated some great quarterbacks who went on to fame and fortune in the pros. The way it is, I guess, bright guys don't take games seriously.

Heinie said, "Last time I saw Mike, he couldn't even pay for his beer. I wonder who popped for his funeral?"

I shrugged.

"Maybe I could spit on him from here?"

"Maybe. It didn't cost me much. He'll be cremated. There won't be any expensive casket."

Heinie sighed. "No open casket, that's for sure. I didn't tell you how he was killed, did I?"

"You didn't."

"A shotgun. Buckshot. Point-blank. Right in the face."

"Jesus!"

"Mary and Joseph," he added.

"He was my roomie for two years at Stanford."

"I didn't know that. Brock, you're not going to get involved in this, are you?"

"I'm not sure."

"Don't be a damned fool! You're too young to die."

"So was Mike. I don't want to talk about it, Heinie."

"Okay, okay! Gad, you are bull-headed," he said, and we rode the rest of the way in silence.

There were seven cars on the mortuary parking lot. There were eight men and three women gathered in the small room off the foyer to pay their final respects to Michael Dennis Gregory. We were the last to arrive.

The man who delivered the eulogy was obviously not a cleric. Heinie was frowning and muttering to himself as the man droned on and on about destiny and space and the Great Beyond. He was either an astronomer or a cultist or a visitor from some other planet.

I hadn't recognized any mourners in the room; all I had seen were the back of their heads. There was a tall, thin, well-dressed man standing next to my car when we got to the parking lot. It had stopped raining. The sun was out.

"Remember me?" he asked.

I shook my head.

"I figured this had to be your car," he said. "There aren't that many classic 1965 Mustangs still running. I was a friend of Mike's. My name is Joe Nolan."

I smiled. *Now* I remember. The big loser."

He nodded. "Poker has never been my game." He took a breath. "I was wondering—are you still a private investigator?"

"I still have my license. But that's not why I'm here. I retired a couple of years ago."

"In San Valdesto, right?"

"Right. What's on your mind, Joe?"

He looked at Heinie and back at me. "It's—kind of private." He looked at Heinie again. "No offense intended. I know you were also a friend of Mike's."

"I'll sit in the car," Heinie said. "I don't want

any part of this." He got in the car and slammed the door.

Nolan said, "What I have to tell you is—oh—kind of complicated. It might not be important. Are you going home tonight?"

I shook my head.

"Where are you staying?"

"At the Beverly Hills Hotel."

"I'll phone you there tonight."

"Do that."

In the car, Heinie was scowling. "You know what Nolan is, don't you?"

"Nope."

"An effing stockbroker, the lowest form of animal life."

Heinie has a sad financial history of investing in junk bonds. I said, "They're not *all* crooks, Heinie."

"Too many are. Let's move. I'm hungry."

I had lunch with him at his bar and grille: sirloin steak, French fries, and two beakers of Einlicher, courtesy of my occasionally gracious host. After an hour of yacking with the Dodger fans in attendance, I drove to the hotel.

I phoned our housekeeper, Mrs. Casey, from there. She told me Jan's plane had taken off on time and asked if I would be home tonight.

I would be visiting friends, I lied, for a few days. Mrs. Casey does not approve of the amateur sleuthing I had returned to in my retirement. She had given up on her crusade to lure me back into "The Only True Church." It is her devout belief that a non-Catholic Irishman is like a fish out of water.

I tried to remember back to the Saturday-night

poker sessions in my former office. As I remembered them, Nolan had not been a regular. Mike had been working at E.F. Hutton then; perhaps that was where they had met.

The life of an informant is hazardous. He is both useful to and despised by the police. He is both hated and despised by the lawless. That last would be the logical choice for Mike's killer. I doubted that even a rogue cop would use a shotgun loaded with buckshot at point-blank range.

The *Los Angeles Times* I bought at the hotel had the story on an inside page. Mike's body had been discovered on the beach in Santa Monica, near the Venice border. Several neighbors, when questioned, had told the police they had heard the blast of the shot. But they had not gone out to investigate. At two o'clock in the morning, in that neighborhood, who could blame them?

But Mike? It was hard for me to believe he was dumb enough to meet anybody, legal or illegal, in *that* area at two o'clock in the morning. That was a dangerous place for an informant, which I had to assume Mike still was.

I phoned the Santa Monica Police Department and asked for Sergeant Lars Hovde. I was informed by the desk sergeant that he was not available at the moment. I gave her my name and phone number and asked that she have Lars phone me as soon as he was available.

The phone rang less than two minutes later. "Where the hell were you; in the toilet?" I asked him.

"I get a lot of nothing calls," he explained. "I'd be on the phone all day if I answered them. What are you doing in town?"

"I came down for Mike Gregory's funeral. You still single?"

"Temporarily. What's on your mind?"

"I thought maybe I could buy you an expensive dinner and we could discuss the murder. Any suspects?"

"None yet. Not that it's any of your business."

"Okay. Buy your own dinner. Who needs *you?*"

"Brock!"

"You ornery bastard," I said, and hung up.

The phone rang seconds later. He said, "Since you left this town, my jock friend, we have a new lieutenant in homicide who *hates* private eyes."

"Okay. I won't invite him to the dinner."

"You win," he said wearily. "Where?"

"Right here at the Beverly Hills Hotel."

"I'll be there at seven," he said. "I get off at six."

Good old Lars, two hundred and fifty pounds of Norwegian out of Minnesota, a welcome addition at any poker table, a man who draws to inside straights and three-card flushes. He was also a welcome addition to any police department. He knew his lacks, so relied on his instincts, the same as I did. He had served in other police departments before moving to Santa Monica. He was not an officer who got along very well with his superiors.

It was a few minutes short of four o'clock when Joe Nolan phoned. He had sorted out his priorities, he said, and decided to tell me what he suspected.

"But," he added, "I have reasons for not informing the police. It might hurt some innocent people, one of whom is one of my clients."

"I see. Are you still with Hutton?"

"No. I opened my own office six years ago."

I told him about my dinner date with Lars and suggested, "Why don't you come over now. You can tell me what you suspect. And if you decide to stay for dinner we—"

"I won't be staying for dinner," he interrupted. "I'll be there in fifteen minutes. My office isn't far from the hotel."

He knocked on the door fifteen minutes later, still looking doubtful.

"Should I order up a couple of drinks?" I asked.

He shook his head. "I'm in AA, like Mike was. He must have been in and out a dozen times. He was out when Hutton had to fire him, the damned fool!"

I nodded. "Booze and broads, those were Mike's failings. I suppose there are worse."

"I guess." He went over to sit in a chair near the window. "That man who delivered the eulogy is a client of mine. I don't know what his original name was. He now calls himself Turhan Bay."

"Like the old movie actor, Turhan Bey?"

"B-a-y, not B-e-y. Maybe that's where he got it. Anyway, he runs a cult called Inner Peace and is doing very well financially. What his congregation doesn't know and wouldn't tolerate, he is also sharing bed and board with a former hooker named Crystal Lane. Do you remember her?"

"Yes. She was one of Mike's girlfriends. But she wasn't a hooker then, so far as I know."

He shrugged. "So far as we both know." He took a deep breath and stared at the floor.

He looked at me. "Add it up. Maybe Mike knew earlier, or later learned about Crystal. And wouldn't Turhan's followers desert the flock if they learned? Wouldn't Mike have strong grounds for a blackmail threat?"

I shook my head. "Not Mike. Never. No!"

"You didn't know him, Brock, in the last few years. He was into drugs then—and they cost money."

"That I didn't know."

"Do you see my dilemma?" he asked. "If I give this to the police, Turhan could find out and I'd lose a million-dollar account." His smile was dim. "I may worship in the temple of Mammon, but I still like to think of myself as a responsible citizen. Whatever your current rates are, I'd be glad to pay them."

"I no longer work for pay," I said. "Mike was my friend."

"Be tactful now, Brock, if you decide to investigate."

"Of course. Tact is my middle name."

He smiled. "What a change!"

On that cynical note, he left. An effing broker is what Heinie had called him. Nolan *might* be one of the better ones.

Suppositions, suppositions, facts not in evidence, as the defense attorneys love to declaim. But it was an avenue of inquiry, the bread and butter of private eyes.

I had left San Valdesto very early this morning to avoid the freeway traffic; I was bushed. It was still two hours short of dinnertime. I stretched out on the bed for a nap.

An hour later I woke up, wet with sweat. I had dreamed of my father again. He had died when I was a kid, killed by a hoodlum, a man who was out on probation for the fourth time.

I took a long warm shower and then a cool one. I dressed and read the sports and business sections of the *Times*. Then I went down to the lobby to wait for Lars.

He looked kind of spiffy when he showed. He was even wearing a tie, one of those William Tell bow ties that columnist George Will favors.

"You put on weight, huh?" was his opening remark.

"Almost two pounds since my playing days," I admitted. "Anything new since last we talked?"

He shook his head. "Mike is not exactly a priority item at the Department right now."

"And with you?"

"Let's have a drink," he said.

Over our drinks, he told me, "You left town before Mike went the last ugly mile. So it's possible that you're more sold on him than I am. You probably didn't know that he wound up on drugs."

"Lars, this town is loaded with highly admired and influential citizens who sniff cocaine at all their fancy parties."

"Hell, yes! But do they also sell it?"

"I don't know. Did Mike?"

He shrugged. "How else can a poor man support his habit if he doesn't deal or steal?"

Facts not in evidence again. I said, "Pretend you're not a cop. Pretend you really care about what happens to victims. Are you telling me to forget what a close friend to both of us Mike was?"

He glowered at me. "God damn you, I liked the guy! But every day we deal with drunks, child molesters, rapists, con men, murderers, burglars, and robbers. And you sit up there in San Valdesto living high off the hog on your inheritance."

"Guilty," I said, and smiled at him. "Another drink?"

He sighed and smiled back at me. "You bastard! I'll have another double. I apologize for the crack about your money. If anybody deserves it, you do."

It went better after that. We traveled down memory lane, recounting old friends and enemies —and where were they all today?

I didn't mention what Nolan had told me. Maybe later . . . He promised to keep me informed on the progress (if any) on Mike's murder investigation but repeated that it was *not* a high priority item to the SMPD.

Then he went home to his woman of the month and I went up to my lonely bed.

CHAPTER TWO

There was a faint tinge of smog in the room when I awoke in the morning. The worst of it, according to the bedside radio, was a second-stage alert in the San Fernando Valley. Santa Monica and Venice, where I planned to prowl this morning, were relatively clear.

I had checked the phone book last night and learned that the cult called Inner Peace was in Venice. That was also where Denny's Tavern was, a knowledgeable source of information for any chicanery that was going on in the area.

The tavern was in an old brick building of three floors, the second and third floors inhabited by Denny and his wife.

Most bars don't open early in the morning. But Denny had another source of income, booking horse bets. He got the blue-collar trade, early-morning bettors on their way to work.

He had been a jockey at one time, but ridden too many horses that finished out of the money. The way he had figured it, there had to be a better way to make a living from the nags.

He smiled as I walked in. "Last time I saw you some guy was trying to ace you. He must have hit a rock, huh?"

That was the nickname my teammates had given me, Brock the Rock. Good beer and bad puns, that's Denny.

I made no comment.

"Beer?" he asked. "I now serve Einlicher. On tap!"

I shook my head. "Too early. Maybe some coffee?"

"Instant?"

"Is that all you have?"

He nodded.

"Then forget it. I came to town for Mike Gregory's funeral. Do you remember him?"

"Hell, yes. He died owing me a thirty-eight-dollar tab. I planned to go to his funeral yesterday, but my wife was ailing and I had to watch the store."

I put two twenties on the bar. "Now he doesn't owe you."

He shook his head. "Forget it."

"Denny," I said, "you take this money or I'll tell the law how you once threw a race at Hollywood Park."

He smiled. "You wouldn't and we both know it. But as long as you are now a rich man—" He picked up the twenties and handed me two singles.

"Did Mike come here often?"

"He did. He spent a lot more than the thirty-eight dollars in this place. Rich one day and poor the next, that was Mike."

"Do you mean lately?"

"Not lately, no. Is that why you're still in town? You playing cops and robbers again?"

"If I have to. Do you know a man named Turhan Bay?"

"The name I know, the man I don't. A weirdo, right?"

"I guess. How about a woman named Crystal Lane?"

He shook his head.

"There is a rumor floating around that Mike might have been involved in selling drugs. Did you hear it?"

"Hell, no! Buying, maybe. But selling? Where would he get the money?"

"Denny, if he could afford to buy, he must have got the money somewhere. A lot of addicts are peddlers. They need to sell in order to support their habit."

"Right. The way I always felt about Mike, he was his own worst enemy. But I find it hard to believe that he'd sink low enough to scout for new victims for the dealers."

That was my gut feeling, too. But it was possible that he might have only switched long-term addicts to a new cheaper source. That could be rationalized as an act of mercy. Mike, like all losers, was prone to rationalization.

"Denny," I said, "nobody knows this neighborhood as well as you do. You would be doing me a big favor if you would find out all you can about Turhan Bay."

"I'll ask around." He smiled. "At least thirty-eight dollars' worth. Play it cool now, Brock. Don't go off half cocked."

"I won't."

I was halfway to the door when he asked, "How about that kook who was out to get you?"

"He's dead," I said.

According to my reckoning, the Temple of Inner Peace was only about two blocks from here. I left the car in Denny's parking lot. My aged Mustang had been stripped in this area the last time I had ventured here. I noticed in the first block that the area had been upgraded since my last visit. But I could use the exercise.

The building looked like a deserted church, complete with cross and steeple. The wide double doorway was up two steps under an arched entrance. A poster on one of the doors informed the faithful that the subject of tonight's lecture was "Inner Peace and Outer Space." Cocaine could give you inner peace and take you to outer space. Was that his pitch? It was difficult to believe that Bay could amass a million-dollar account with Joe Nolan by lecturing to the residents of Venice.

A white-haired elderly woman in a brightly flowered dress was sitting at a card table in the foyer.

"May I help you?" she asked.

"I hope so. I was at a funeral yesterday where your minister gave the eulogy. The man who died was a friend of mine years ago. I have learned since that he had gone into a deep depression recently."

She frowned. "Are you speaking of Michael Gregory?"

I nodded.

"I hope you aren't suggesting that he committed suicide. He was murdered!"

"That," I said, "is what the police claim—murdered with a shotgun. They also claim that they found no weapon near the body. I lived in Santa Monica for twelve years and have good cause to believe they were lying."

She stared at me.

"What's your minister's name?" I asked.

"He's not really—a—a minister," she said. "His name is Turhan Bay. He won't be here until this afternoon. Could I have him phone you?"

"No, I'll get in touch with him."

"Your name?"

"Carlton Ramsay."

"Mr. Gregory was not a member of our flock," she said, "but he was a very close friend of Turhan's and Turhan tried to help him."

"That's what I've been told. I look forward to meeting him."

Millionaire electronic preachers and kooky cults were infesting our country. Maybe Mrs. Casey was right; it was time to return to the true church. But what about confession? How could I convince the priest that incessant lying was a requisite of my trade. It was a necessary evil, designed to keep the bad guys discombobulated.

There were a pair of teenagers standing next to my Mustang when I came back to the parking lot. They looked normal enough, but who can tell, these days?

Then one of them said, "A sixty-fiver, right? Two hundred and eighty-nine cubes?"

I nodded. "Right. With a four-barrel carb and Spelke cams."

"What'll she do?" his partner asked.

I shrugged. "I've never had her over a hundred. I'm too old and too frail to test her above that."

"You don't look frail to me," he said.

"How about old?"

It was his turn to shrug. "Oh, maybe thirty, thirty-two?"

"You have just earned yourself a pair of Cokes," I said, and handed him a fin.

"Thank you, sir!" he said, and the two of them went into Denny's.

Maybe for a few beers? No. Denny was strict

about that. There was still hope for the future of the planet.

From there to the SMPD. The desk sergeant told me Lars was out on the street and would be all day. But it was possible, he added, that I could catch him around noon at Ye Sandwich Shoppe on Wilshire. Lars usually ate his lunch there.

It was still short of eleven o'clock. I used the phone book in the hall to see if there was a listing for Crystal Lane. There was, 332 Adonis Court. I knew the street, a short one, and not in the high-rent district.

They were all small frame houses on a narrow dead-end street. On the pitted asphalt driveway of 332, a sleek black Jaguar was parked. I wrote down the license number before I went up the one step porch to ring the doorbell.

No answer. I rang again. The same. I went back to the car to sit and wait. It seemed highly unlikely to me that the Jag was Crystal's. How long could they fornicate?

Too long for me. A few minutes before noon I drove to Ye Sandwiche Shoppe. Lars walked in soon after.

"You bought the dinner," he said. "I'll buy the lunch. I suppose you've been sticking your big nose into police business all morning."

"Somebody has to." I didn't reveal my sources, but I told him what I had learned from Denny and Joe Nolan, and what I had suspected at my stakeout at Crystal's house.

"You've got that Turhan-Lane bit wrong," he informed me. "They're not shacked up together. Turhan lives in Brentwood."

"Does he drive a Jaguar?"

Lars shrugged. "I don't know."

I handed him the slip. "Here's the license number of the Jag that was parked on Crystal's driveway."

"I'll check it out." He took a deep breath. "I picked up Miss Lane a few times when I was working Vice a few years ago. But I sure as hell can't pick her up for having an expensive car on her driveway."

"You picked her up for prostitution?"

"Yup. But she had some expensive clients and beat the rap."

"Did you know that she was once Mike's girlfriend?"

He shook his head. "Are you suggesting that Turhan Bay was involved in Mike's murder?"

"Maybe, maybe not. He gave the eulogy at Mike's funeral."

"That's really weird, Brock! Where's the connection?"

I shrugged.

"The funeral was in Westwood," he said. "That's outside of our jurisdiction. So is Brentwood, where Bay lives, and so is Venice, where he runs his con. The LA Westside Station is where you should go with your weird theories."

"I'm not welcome there. They remember me from the old days."

"That was before you moved. Tell 'em you're rich now."

I sighed. "You are one cynical bastard, Lars."

He didn't answer, munching away at his double cheeseburger. I gave my attention to my more refined avocado-and-bacon sandwich on rye toast.

Over our coffee, I said, "Bay is giving a lecture

tonight on inner peace and outer space. It might be interesting. Would you like to come with me?"

"I don't work nights."

"It wouldn't be work. Maybe it would help you attain inner peace. You could use some of that."

"Watch it, acid tongue!"

"Screw you!" I finished my coffee and stood up. "Thanks for the lunch."

"Dear God, now we get the petulance bit. I'll check that license number and phone you. When will you be back at the hotel?"

"Around five."

"I'll phone you there."

I smiled down at him. "Thanks. Buddies again, Lars?"

"Hell, yes," he said, "but I don't know why."

Two hours later, after a fruitless search of my former informants in the area, I drove to the hotel and put in a long-distance call to Tacoma. Jan answered.

"I'm still in smog town," I told her, "and I miss you."

"I'll bet you do! With all those bimbos you used to know down there?"

"Jan, I had lunch with one cynic today and one is more than enough."

"What's her name?"

"Lars Hovde. Remember him?"

"That big man from Minnesota, that Santa Monica detective?"

"That's the man. How are things in Tacoma?"

"Not so good. Aunt Alice has a cold and needs a lot of rest. I may come home a little later than we'd planned. You are *not* going to get involved in that murder, are you?"

"I'm not sure."

"Brock—!"

"I'll say one thing and then we will drop the subject. Mike Gregory was my friend."

"And fellow womanizer."

I considered reminding her that she was not a virgin when we first met, but decided not to.

About a half minute of silence from Tacoma and then she said, "I apologize. I can be bitchy, can't I?"

"It's one of your charms. I adore you, feisty."

"It's mutual. You keep that fly of yours zipped shut."

"Even in the toilet?"

That got a laugh out of her. Then, "Aunt Alice is coughing again. I have to go. You be very careful down there!"

"I will. That's a promise."

CHAPTER THREE

Lars phoned a few minutes after five o'clock. The Jaguar, he told me, was listed as the property of Turhan Bay. "Now maybe you can tell me what the connection is with Mike's murder."

I told him the theory held by Nolan.

"You're reaching, aren't you? Did one of your brainwashed stoolies feed you that script?"

"Nope. I dreamed it up all by myself."

"Blackmail? Mike—?"

"It could be a bad script. The lady at the Inner Peace place told me that Bay was a very close friend of Mike's and tried to help him. What I can't believe is that he would try to help anybody who couldn't afford to pay him."

"Not unless he had reason to."

"He could have reason. Blackmail could be a strong reason for a man as broke as Mike. Mike didn't even belong to that kooky outfit. And we both know a heavy habit needs heavy money."

"That makes sense," he admitted.

"And," I pointed out, "it's not outside your jurisdiction. Mike died in Santa Monica."

"Okay, okay," he said wearily. "I'll ask around."

"Thanks, Lars. Give my best to your latest."

"Latest what?"

"Female conquest," I said, and hung up.

I hadn't planned to sit through tonight's lecture. My hope was that I could talk privately with Bay and sort of test the way the wind was blowing.

The lecture was scheduled for eight o'clock. I phoned at six-thirty and a woman answered. I gave her my phony name and asked if she remembered my visit.

"I certainly do, Mr. Ramsay," she said.

"Could I speak with Turhan tonight before the lecture?"

"He will be here at seven."

The black Jaguar was on the small parking lot that flanked the temple. I parked next to it.

There was no one in the foyer. I walked down the middle aisle past the rows of benches. There was a closed door in the wall next to the rostrum and voices from behind it. I knocked. The woman I had talked with that morning opened the door.

"Come in," she said. And to Bay, "This is Carlton Ramsay."

He was standing behind his desk, a thin, fairly tall man with cold blue eyes. He said, "Have a seat, Mr. Ramsay," and nodded at the woman.

She left and closed the door. I sat in a straight chair near his desk.

He stared at me for a few seconds. "That was a strange story you told my secretary this morning. Why would the Santa Monica police claim Mike was murdered if he wasn't?"

"It's possible that he was. It is also possible that he committed suicide. And that is what I hope to clear up. Do you believe he was despondent enough to take his own life?"

"I do."

"Do you think he did?"

He shrugged. "That's what I don't understand. No weapon was found."

"Not *yet*," I said. "Mr. Bay, I worked for the

38

Arden Investigative Service in Santa Monica for twelve years. I finally had to leave the town and the agency. I uncovered some shenanigans that were going on in the Department and was harassed constantly by them after that."

He smiled. "And now you are on a vindictive crusade? That is a waste of time and effort. They have the clout in court and they are the law."

I agreed with a nod. "And if you think Mike could have committed suicide—?" I took a breath. "But I remember the riot guns the Department used in those days. They were sawed-off shotguns and that was the kind of weapon that probably blew away Mike's face."

He stared at me. "Are you suggesting that—"

"I'm not suggesting anything, Mr. Bay. You've learned all that I know. I want to thank you for the help you tried to give Mike and your kind words about him in your eulogy."

I heard the door open behind me and turned. And there she stood in the open doorway, a shade heavier and a touch older, but as beautiful as ever —Crystal Lane.

She smiled at me. "Brock Callahan, as I live and breathe! It's been a long time, honey boy."

I brushed past her and hurried down the aisle. I was in the car, feeling like a country bumpkin, when Crystal came out the front door. She shouted something I couldn't understand. I didn't stop.

My current investigative techniques were no longer as sharp as they should be. Soft living and too many misspent hours on the golf course in San Valdesto had obviously dulled them.

I stopped at Denny's for a glass of Einlicher. He had, he told me, asked around about Bay this afternoon and got a lot of mixed reports on the man. He seemed to have gained favor with the women in the neighborhood, but was not generally admired by the men. I told him where I had been and what had happened.

Denny sighed. "Have you ever thought of retiring, Brock?"

"Not until tonight."

The man standing next to me at the bar, a large man in cheap clothes, said, "Brock? Brock the Rock?"

Denny nodded.

"You were the greatest," the man said. "Can I shake your hand?"

We shook hands.

"This Turhan Bay you mentioned, is he a friend of yours?"

"No way! Do you know him?"

He shook his head. "But the wife thinks he's God. She's down there right now, listening to his bullshit. He's really making a lot of money with his blarney. I told the wife if she wanted to contribute to that creep she'd have to take it out of her household money."

Denny smiled. "I'll bet you haven't been eating too good since then."

"No bet," the man said. "Brock, if you ever tangle with that weirdo, give him an extra shot for me."

I promised him I would, my ego restored.

A few beers and two hours of jock talk after that, I left. The night was clear, the stars were bright. I drove slowly and carefully to 332 Adonis Court and turned on the car radio to a local big band station.

A few minutes after ten o'clock, an ancient but

40

still glossy Volkswagen Bug came down the street and pulled into the driveway. Crystal got out to open the garage door. I left my car before she got back into hers.

"You dumb jock," she said. "Why did you take off like that? I explained to Turhan that you were just having fun with him. You were never very good at the con, muscles."

"I was doing pretty well at it until you opened your big mouth. How long have you been sleeping with him?"

"Turhan sleeps at home, smartass. In *this* house it's *all* business."

"I know. Lars told me that."

"Lars Hovde?"

I nodded.

"He should talk! He's probably slept with every woman in town except for maybe the mayor's wife."

"Crystal, let's not fight."

"Okay. Wait for me on the porch. We'll have a cup of coffee for auld lang syne and talk about better times and nicer people."

The front door opened directly into the living room. It was a very small house, badly furnished in discount house moderne.

I sat in a plastic-upholstered armchair; she went into the kitchen. If Turhan was raking in the loot he certainly wasn't sharing it with her. I mentioned this when she brought us our coffee.

She frowned. "Loot? What loot? In Venice?"

"The word I got, the man is rich."

She shook her head. "His wife is rich. And *old!*"

"Did she buy him the Jaguar?"

"She did. And he bought me the Bug. Brock, so help me, the man really believes what he's selling."

"I'm not sure what he's selling," I said. "I couldn't make any sense out of his talk at the mortuary."

She shrugged. "He's not for everybody."

"You and Mike," I said. "If you'll excuse my sentimentality, I always thought you two were meant for each other."

"Maybe it would have worked out if he had some sense of reality, an instinct for an honest dollar. If we'd have married, I'm sure we would have wound up on welfare. Brock, it's easy to be moral when you inherit a fortune."

I smiled at her. "Your round. I apologize. What I can't believe is that Mike would sink low enough to peddle dope."

"I don't know that he did. Do you?"

"Not for sure. Does Bay?"

"If he did, he never mentioned it to me. He tried his damnedest to get Mike off the stuff. Mike destroyed himself, Brock."

I nodded. " 'A million dollars of promise worth two cents on delivery.' "

"What does that mean?"

"It's a line from a book by Mark Harris. Mike could have made a good living, even in those days, as a pro quarterback."

"Maybe. You had a pro career and wound up as a private eye in a two-bit office. Tell me—if your uncle Homer hadn't died where would you have wound up?"

"Still in the two-bit office," I admitted. "Let's talk about better times and nicer people."

Which we did.

When I got up to leave, she said, "Keep in touch, huh?"

I nodded.

"I suppose you're still happily married?"

"Unfortunately, yes," I said.

Nolan had told me it was Bay who had the big-money account at his office. Now Crystal had told me it was his wife who was rich. Both could be right; it was possible they had a joint account. In this chauvinistic world, the husband's name was always the top name on a joint brokerage or bank account. Jan had pointed that out to me soon after we were married.

I thought of phoning her when I came back to the hotel, to learn how her aunt was doing, but decided against it. Late-night phone calls are too often frightening to the callee.

I recorded the things I had been told today and the things I suspected, trying to find a pattern. I had no way of knowing how many of the things I had been told were lies. When I learned which of them were, it should help to narrow the search.

CHAPTER FOUR

Nolan had told me that Bay had a big account at his brokerage. Crystal had told me that Bay's wife had the money. Both stories could be true—or false.

Because of the time zones, brokers in California had to come to work a lot earlier than those in New York. I phoned Nolan before breakfast and told him what Crystal had told me.

Mrs. Bay, he informed me, was still with E.F. Hutton and had been for many years. He said, "I hope you didn't mention to Crystal what I told you about Bay's account. It is none of her damned business!"

"I didn't mention it and I won't," I promised.

"Brock, I don't want you to mention it to *anybody*. That is why I was so hesitant about telling you what I did. I went out on a limb for you because of the way we both feel about Mike."

"I appreciate it, Joe," I said, and hung up.

A stockbroker with both a heart and ethics? He could be unique.

I had breakfast at the hotel and went to my room. The morning was gloomy and overcast and I had nowhere to go.

What Nolan had just told me was added to the record. No pattern emerged. If Crystal had told the truth about Bay's slim pickings in Venice, he had to have another source of income. And if Nolan knew that it came from a doubtful source, he could be in big trouble with the SEC. If he pried into it and Bay learned that he had, it could lose him the Bay account. That put him between a rock and a hard place.

The morning *Times* financial page reported that two more of our eminently respectable brokerage houses were now under investigation by the Feds for illegal insider trading. Maybe Joe had called it right; he had gone out on a limb. But not for me.

I was learning nothing here in the room. At eleven-thirty I drove out to Ye Sandwich Shoppe in the hope that Lars would show.

On my second cup of coffee, he walked in. He looked sour.

"Don't sulk," I said. "I'm buying today."

"It's been a bad morning," he said. "Anything new by you?"

I shook my head. "Nothing important." I told him about my trip to the temple last night and what Bay had told me before Crystal walked in and made me look even more foolish than usual.

He ordered a beer and sipped in silence. After several minutes I asked, "What's bugging you, buddy?"

"For one thing," he said, "my job. I'm still six years short of pension time and still a sergeant. And today I learned that a kinky killer I put away is now out on parole. Maybe you remember him?"

"Maybe if you tell me his name."

"Carlo Minatti, known in the trade as Kooky Carl. Do you remember him?"

I shook my head. "Italian. Mafia?"

"Nope. Strictly independent. This I need in my declining years? Jesus, Brock, I've been a sergeant for twelve years and they aren't going to let me get any higher, not in this town, not with Slade in charge."

I said nothing.

Over our sandwiches he said, "The way I see it, I'm going to have to get to him before he gets to me. And then, about an hour ago, I remembered something else. His favorite weapon was a sawed-off shotgun."

"You think he might be the man who blasted Mike?"

"I doubt it. But he could be. He was always for hire."

"I'll go along with you this afternoon," I said.

"Don't be silly! You're not even carrying, are you?"

"No. I didn't have any reason to bring my ancient Colt .45 down here just for the funeral. We'll take my car. It doesn't smell of cop."

"And you are not a cop."

"Right. But this Minatti could be the man we're both looking for."

He studied me for seconds before he finally said, "Okay."

Lars has this theory that male convicts who have been on a restricted diet of pederasty in jail hunger for a return to female company when they are released. And female informants are usually less stubborn than males. The first two female stops were fruitless. When he told me to head for Venice, I reminded him that Venice was out of his jurisdiction.

"Not today," he said. "I'm off the clock. This one is personal."

Which could get him into a lot of trouble. I didn't voice the thought.

We made three stops in Venice, all of which were likewise fruitless. Then we headed for Denny's.

Why, I wondered, would a man who just got out after a long stretch in prison risk going back in? I was assuming that Minatti could be the man who killed Mike. I voiced the thought to Lars.

"Because," he explained, "they have to eat and pay rent, just like us solid citizens. What other trade do they know?"

"Did you question his parole officer?"

"He's the man who alerted me. Minatti missed a visit this week and he had moved from the original address he gave the officer."

Denny was laying out ten-dollar bills on the bar to an enormous black man in an expensive suit when we walked in.

They both turned to stare at us. Denny smiled and said, "Just paying the rent, boys."

Lars smiled back at him. "Of course. We're here for the Einlicher."

Denny laid the last tenner on the bar and the man walked out. He went to the tap and poured us two beakers. "On the house," he said. "There were two guys in here asking about you this afternoon, Brock."

"Asking what?"

"They wanted to know where you were staying in town. One of them left his card." He took a card from the back bar and handed it to me.

Dennis Sadler, the card read: *Arden Investigative Services.* My lie to Turhan Bay had come back to haunt me.

I handed the card to Lars and told him the story I had fed Turhan Bay.

"This one is in my jurisdiction," he said. "We'll drop in on the way back and straighten them out."

Another beer later we did. The head man at Arden was short and pudgy. I have forgotten his name. He explained to us patiently that Arden *never* revealed the name of a client.

Lars flashed his badge and said, "We know his name, that freak who runs that crazy cult. What I'm here to find out is why your stooges are harassing Mr. Callahan."

The little man glared at Lars. "My agents are not stooges and I do not consider an investigation a harassment."

"And I suppose you don't consider Mr. Bay a con man?"

"I certainly do not, and neither does my wife. And as for your friend there, he lied about his identity and in his statement that he used to work for this agency."

Lars smiled. "Are you trying to tell me that none of your agents has ever been guilty of lying?"

"No more than your friend has. I remember him now. He had a one-man office in Beverly Hills some years ago."

Lars nodded. "He did. But aren't we all on the same side of the law? You can't possibly believe that Bay is."

"I do, and so does my wife."

"And did Bay ever tell you about his previous pseudonyms?"

"I don't know he had any. Could you name them?"

Lars shook his head. "That would be Department business. But, for your information, he had several."

The little man glared at us as we went out. He was still glaring when I closed the door.

Lars was chuckling. "What a con man, right?"

"There were three of us in the room," I said, "including one police officer. When did you dream up that pseudonym bit?"

"It was only a ploy. I wanted to keep that little bastard off balance."

When I dropped him off at the station, he gave me the picture of Minatti he had been carrying for identification to his informants. "Maybe you'll have more luck," he explained.

I stopped on the way back to the hotel to see if Crystal was home. The garage door was open and the garage empty. I rang her bell three times with no response.

For a girl who had inhabited some luxurious suites and impressive homes, the cheaply furnished cottage had to be a depressing comedown. Crystal was flighty, but not dumb, and she had a sound regard for the dollar. It was unlikely that she shared the belief of the little man at Arden regarding Turhan Bay. Honest and dedicated men were not her quarry—unless they were also rich. Bay, she had claimed, was not.

There was nothing to add to the record except for the shotgun hit-man item. I would remember that without recording it.

I ate dinner at the hotel and came back to the room with no place to go. The Dodgers were playing the Giants in San Francisco on the boob tube. The Giants were ahead, 10 to 2, in the eighth inning when I turned off the set and went to bed.

The morning *Times* reported that another brokerage house was under investigation on information furnished by former culprits. Even the dignified denizens of Wall Street were turning into stoolies.

I was walking through the lobby, heading for breakfast, when the desk clerk gestured to me. When I came within earshot, he said, "I just phoned your room. That man sitting next to the entrance asked for you. Shall I tell him you are here?"

"Don't bother. *I'll* tell him."

He was a young man, probably under thirty, in gray slacks and a dark-gray blazer, a yuppie type.

"Mr. Callahan?" he asked, and stood up.

I nodded.

"My name is Dennis Sadler," he said.

"I recognize it. You are the Dennis who left his card at Denny's. How did you learn I was staying here?"

He smiled. "Mr. Callahan, I may be young but I am not incompetent. The boss told me the officer who was with you yesterday claimed to know Turhan Bay's former pseudonyms. Was that true?"

"I don't know," I lied. "And if I did, I don't think I should tell anyone but the police."

"As you wish." He smiled again. "I know his original name."

"Have you had breakfast?" I asked.

He nodded. "But I could use a cup of coffee if you're buying. Arden doesn't pay much."

"I'm buying."

Over my eggs, toast, and bacon and his cup of coffee, he told me how it was. His mother-in-law was an ardent Bay believer, contributing much more than she could afford. He had done his research through a former schoolmate in Chicago, where he had grown up, and learned that Bay had run a phony money market scam with promises of a twenty-four percent annual return. He had concentrated on rich and gullible widows.

"Did he do any time?"

"Only six months on probation. One of the widows still believed in him. She helped to pay off the victims." He paused. "Didn't you used to work this area?"

I nodded.

"Does the name Terrible Tim Tucker ring a bell?"

"Dimly. Isn't he a wrestler, one of those groan-and-grunt freaks?"

"That's the man. And later he was a muscle man for several Los Angeles bookies, the collector. I'm not sure, but the rumor is that he has gone even heavier since. Turhan Bay is his cousin. Bay's real name is Gordon Tucker."

"Thanks, Dennis. You've really done your homework."

"Oh, yes! But not enough to convince my mother-in-law." He took a card out of his wallet and handed it to me. "That's my home phone number. I do some free-lancing when I'm off duty. I'll never get rich at Arden."

"I'll keep you in mind," I promised. "And thanks again."

CHAPTER FIVE

I phoned the Santa Monica station and Lars was there. I told him what Sadler had told me, except for the mother-in-law complaint.

He confirmed what Sadler had suspected; Terrible Tim Tucker had moved up from his collector days. He was now a bodyguard for any minor-league hoodlum who hoped to move up to the majors.

"We ran him out of this town," he told me. "I have no idea where he is operating now. I'll ask around and let you know if I learn anything."

There was no Tim Tucker listed in any of the hotel phone books. I knew a man who might help me. I drove to The Captain's Gym, run by the venerable Captain Robert Napier, on Olympic Boulevard near the Olympic Auditorium.

The odor of perspiration was strong when I entered. A pair of ugly showmen were practicing winning and losing in the center ring, complete with scowls, fist shaking, and vulgar verbal insults.

The odor in Napier's small office was a slight improvement, expensive cigar smoke. He was sitting behind his battered desk.

"Callahan," he said, and stood up. "What are you doing in town?"

"I came down for Mike Gregory's funeral. Do you remember him?"

He shook his head. "Is he the guy who was killed in Santa Monica?"

I nodded. "I'm working with the Santa Monica police. Mike was a good friend of mine."

"I thought you left the shamus racket when your uncle died."

"I did. This one is personal. I was wondering if you know a former wrestler named Terrible Tim Tucker."

"That creep? You mean he might be the killer?"

"Possibly, but doubtful. He might be a lead."

He nodded. "The last I heard he was the muscle man for Arnie Gillete. Gillete lives up in the Valley somewhere. I don't know where. Maybe he's in the book."

He reached into a desk drawer and took out a telephone book. "You could look it up. My eyes aren't what they used to be."

It was there—Arnold Gillete on Eureka Drive in Studio City.

"Do you know what Gillete's into now?" I asked.

He shrugged. "Anything that makes him a dirty buck, I suppose. When I first met him, his name was Arno Gilleti. He used to book bets at the Olympic in the old days. Strictly small-time. Did Jan come to town with you?"

"Nope. She's visiting her aunt in Tacoma. How about your lady friend? Did you finally marry her?"

"Gloria? Yup. Eight months ago. Now you and I are both solid citizens. There's nothing like that good home-cooking, right?"

"Right," I said, not mentioning that we had a cook. That would be one-upmanship. I thanked him and left. The behemoths were still practicing winning and losing in the gym. I headed for the San Fernando Valley.

It was hot in the Valley and the air smoggy. The home of Arnold Gillete was low and wide and white, fronted by a large expanse of bright-green dichondra lawn.

There was a four-car parking space at the end of the driveway, occupied by one car, a green Bentley. Arno had apparently graduated to the majors. I parked on the road in front and walked up the drive.

The man who opened the door to my ring looked considerably older than the image of him I had seen on the tube during his wrestling days and later on gymnasium commercials. His dyed white hair was gone; he was bald. But he was as big and ugly as ever.

"You selling something?" he asked.

I shook my head. "I'm trying to locate an old friend of mine from Chicago. I just moved here a week ago and I couldn't find any listing in the phone book."

He glanced back into the house and quietly closed the door behind him. He said, "I'm not in the phone book, either. Who told you I lived here?"

"A wrestler at Muscle Beach. I didn't get his name."

"What's your friend's name?"

"Gordon Tucker. That's why I'm here."

"And your name?"

"Dallas McGee."

He stared at me for seconds. Then, "I don't think so. I know I've seen you somewhere. Let's see your driver's license."

"Are you calling me a liar?"

He nodded. "Let's see your license."

"Get lost!" I said, and turned to go back to the car.

He grabbed me by the right shoulder. I turned and nailed him with a looping right-hand smack on the button. He stumbled to one side. I swung my right foot into his jewel box and he went down, groaning.

I was in the car and driving away before he could get back to his feet. Wrestlers. . . .

One way or another they were all connected: Bay and Tucker and Gillete and Nolan and Mike and possibly Carlos Minatti.

And Crystal. I drove there next. She was out on her driveway in shorts and a halter, her hair in curlers, washing her Bug.

"Dear God, the peeper!" she said. "What now?"

"You told me we should keep in touch."

"You could have picked a better time."

"Okay. I'll leave quietly."

"Stay," she said. "Coffee?"

I nodded.

She turned off the hose and we went into the house. I sat in the Naugahyde chair; she went into her closet-size kitchen. "Maybe some Danish, too?" she asked. "I remember you had a sweet tooth."

"I still have it."

Ten minutes later she brought the coffee and pastry out on a tray, along with two paper napkins. She set up two TV tables, one in front of me, the other in front of her studio couch.

"Ain't we the cozy ones?" she said. "I hope you didn't come with questions."

"A few. Did you know that Bay's real name is Gordon Tucker?"

"I knew it once was. He had it changed. *Legally.*"

"Did you know he spent six months in Chicago for running a crooked financial racket?"

She nodded. "And nobody suffered. Everybody was paid off. He's a different man now, Brock."

I considered adding what Nolan had told me about Bay's account there, but I had promised him I wouldn't.

She smiled at me. "Have you run out of questions?"

"Only of patience," I said wearily. "Do you plan to get married again?"

She was still smiling. "If you get a divorce, I might. I like rich guys."

A bite of Danish, a sip of coffee, and silence.

"Cat got your tongue?" she asked.

"God damn you!" I said. "Mike's murdered and you sit there with that silly smile on your face, talking nonsense."

Her face stiffened, her eyes glazed with moisture. "What do you want me to do, take the veil, burn incense? Your jock friend is dead. And better men than you or Mike have died before their time and many more will. Don't get too damned noble, Callahan. You're not exactly a saint."

Silence—and more of the same. I ate the last bit of roll, drank the rest of my coffee, and stood up. I stared at her and she at me. Then I turned and went out.

The lady had made her point. *Judge not that ye be not judged, Callahan,* I told myself. *You left the church long ago.*

From there I drove to the office of Nolan,

57

Welch, and Ryan. Nolan was there, but getting ready to leave for lunch.

"Something important?" he asked.

I nodded.

"We can discuss it over lunch," he said. And added, "On me."

We ate at a sidewalk cafe under an awning only two short blocks from his office. Over our martinis I asked him if he knew about Bay's probation sentence in Chicago.

He nodded. "He told me all about it, including his change of name. He was quite frank with me and I saw no reason to reject his account. Though I must admit I was nervous about it at the time." He took a sip of his drink. "Frankly, I know of several respectable brokerage houses which I suspect of handling doubtful accounts."

"Did Bay ever tell you that his cousin is a muscle man for Arnold Gillete?"

He stared at me and shook his head. "He never mentioned *any* cousin to me. Who is Arnold Gillete?"

"A local hoodlum."

He smiled. "Isn't that a bit farfetched? I mean— the cousin of my client is working for a hoodlum. Therefore the client should be punished."

"It's overreaching," I admitted. "What I can't figure is how he got big money out of that cult in Venice."

He shrugged. "It's possible he also gets some upper-income followers. Cults seem to be doing well these days."

"Maybe he brought his money from Chicago."

"It's possible. But where he got his money is no business of mine. We don't ask our clients where they got their money. Brock, my only reason for contacting you was the hope that you might learn more about who killed Mike than the Santa Monica Department will. From my brief talk with Chief Denzler there I had the feeling that they were not overly interested in Mike's murder."

"They aren't," I admitted. "But I am."

The Danish was still in my stomach. I had a salad for lunch. Half an hour of small talk after that he went back to work and I back to the hotel to learn if there were any messages for me.

There was one from Lars. I phoned the station and was told he was out for lunch. He would be back at four o'clock.

I added today's semirevelations to the record. All I had were names and connections and no pointing finger. I stretched out on the bed and ran the events of the morning through my mind. I was dozing when Lars phoned.

He had good news. At least it was good news for him. Carlos Minatti had been arrested in Fresno, after robbing a liquor store. That should give him another stretch in prison. And, he added, I could eliminate one name from my favorite suspects list. Minatti had been in Fresno when Mike was killed.

"How about your list, Lars? Mike was our friend."

"I know. But more your friend than mine. Wasn't he the guy who tipped you off when that kook was trying to put you away?"

"He was. I hope Minatti gets a long stretch. You're too young to die, Lars."

"Right!"

"So was Mike," I said, and hung up.

It had been an unrewarding day and I was sour. I

shouldn't have taken that shot at Lars. Day after day on his job he saw only the seamy side of the street. And if Mike hadn't been my savior, I doubt if Heinie would have phoned me. I might never have learned that Mike was dead. It wouldn't be important news to the San Valdesto paper.

A lecture to Crystal and a cheap shot at Lars . . . Maybe I needed a Dale Carnegie course.

I went over my notes again and saw something I had overlooked. When he first came to the hotel, Nolan had told me he didn't know what Bay's original name was. At lunch today he had told me Bay had told him that when he opened his account. What else had he lied about? And had he really learned, or only been told, that Bay was sharing bed and board with Crystal. He had identified her as a former hooker. Where had he learned that, and why? Maybe at his talk with Chief Denzler. And maybe not.

In my hungry years in this town, I had done some divorce work. One of my clients was a broker at Hutton who suspected his wife was backdooring him. I had saved him a considerable amount of alimony.

I looked him up in the book and phoned him at his home number. I identified myself and asked him, "Do you remember me?"

"Until my dying day," he said. "What's on your mind?"

"A man named Joe Nolan."

"He's not with us anymore, Brock."

"I know. I wondered why."

"There were a number of reasons. I guess what you'd call erratic behavior covers them all. The boss called it lying. Joe claimed it was an occasional loss of memory."

"He contradicted himself a couple of times when I talked with him. When he first came to see me, he said he was in AA. Today we had lunch together and he had a martini."

"That's not unusual. I went to a couple of meetings myself. But my shrink convinced me that if I was able to produce the way I have, I was a drunk, not an alcoholic. So I've cut down. One drink a day for the last four years."

"You don't think Nolan's a compulsive liar?"

"Not compulsive. Maybe when he has to be—as *you* should know. He's got a couple of partners who can keep him on track. By the way, now that you're rich, where are you investing your money?"

"With a discount broker."

"Well, next time you need a stoolie, call *him!*"

"Thanks for the info," I said, and hung up.

CHAPTER SIX

Nolan had told me in this room that he had sorted out his priorities and decided to reveal all. Lying had apparently been his first priority. The urge to point this out to him was strong in me, but it would probably only alert him.

Shadowing suspects and wearisome surveillance stakeouts had never been my favorite kind of investigative work. I still had Dennis Sadler's card. I phoned him after dinner and asked if he was available for part-time labor.

"Full-time," he told me. "I have two weeks of vacation due, starting tomorrow."

"Could you drop in tonight for a briefing?"

"I'm on the way."

He brought a small, battery-operated recorder with him. This young man was part of the electronic age. I gave him the cast of characters first, and then their connections. I added my suspicions and admitted they could easily be wrong. And finally I asked him what his rates were.

"Twenty dollars an hour," he said.

"And expenses?"

"Only for gasoline. I don't have any office expense, working out of my house. This Arnold Gillete—he's heavy, isn't he?"

"I'm sure he's not as heavy as his bodyguard, though I've never met Gillete."

"I didn't mean avoirdupois," he said. "What I'm

thinking, my wife doesn't want me to carry a gun. Though I always do when I have guard work."

"I didn't bring my gun with me because I didn't think I would be staying over. If push comes to shove with Gillete, I'll borrow your gun."

When he left, I stretched out on the bed. Fatigue was heavy in me, but I knew I couldn't sleep. It had been a troublesome day, bucking traffic on the way to Studio City, the fuss with Crystal, the sense that I was getting nowhere in my hunt.

Half an hour later, Lars phoned. "Still mad, hothead?"

"I'm sorry, Lars. I apologize."

"You're forgiven. I straightened out our hard-nosed lieutenant today."

"The one who doesn't like private eyes?"

"That's the man. He doesn't even like his own kids. I explained to him, with our slim budget, we should use all the free help we can get. That registered with him. I also told him you were rich. That clinched it. I'll be busy in the morning. Maybe around noon at the sandwich shop?"

"I'll be there."

I put in a call to Tacoma and nobody answered. Jan's aunt was an incurable movie addict. She must have gotten over her cold.

It was a restless night; it was after midnight before I finally fell asleep. The phone awakened me a little after eight o'clock. It was Jan.

"How was the movie?" I asked.

"Are you psychic?"

"Nope. I phoned last night and there was no answer. And I remembered how much your aunt loves movies."

"God, yes." She lowered her voice. "And the

64

worse they are, the better she likes. Tell me honestly, are you behaving yourself in that evil city?"

"I am. I miss you."

"And I you. Have you learned anything about what happened to Mike?"

"Not yet."

"Now, damn it, you be careful!"

"Fear not. I am now officially working with the Santa Monica Police Department."

"That's comforting to hear. I have to hang up. Alice has the sniffles and I'm making her some chicken soup."

The enigma in this case was Joe Nolan. The rest of the cast were not difficult to decipher; their goals were standard, the big buck, the American dream.

Nolan had admitted that the temple of Mammon was his house of worship. He was the only person who had given me information without being asked. He had lied to me twice.

It was also possible that he had lied about the Bay account. But why? I couldn't think of any reason that would tie him up with Mike's murder. A liar he certainly was; it's almost a requisite of his trade. But I couldn't see him as a man who would blow away a man's face with a shotgun at night on the beach. He could be a key to this puzzle, but not the killer.

It was my experience in this nefarious profession that learning the *why* is the surest path to the *who*. This case was shaping up as a whydunit.

My new employee was out on the hunt. Lars would work with me this afternoon. I had run out of informants and places to go. I went back to my notes and the *Times*.

The notes were as inconclusive as they were last night.

The *Times* informed their readers that a financial firm in Thousand Oaks was being investigated by the Securities and Exchange Commission for what was labeled a sham operation—massive stock manipulations which had profited one participant to the tune of eight and a half million dollars.

The participant's attorney would probably wind up with more of the loot than his client or the SEC. It has always been a puzzle to me that the people who can most afford to be honest so rarely are.

On the way to meet Lars I detoured to Crystal's house, hoping to learn if we could be friends again. She wasn't home.

I was in a booth, drinking a diet Coke, when Lars arrived.

"What in the hell is that?" he asked.

"A diet Coke. I have to watch my weight."

He shook his head and sat down across from me. I told him about my one-round victory over Terrible Tim, and Sadler's visit last night.

"That's all we need," he said, "another private eye on the case. The lieutenant could change his mind if he hears about that."

"He doesn't have to know. And none of it is in his jurisdiction." I told him about Nolan's lies. "Sadler will handle that end in Beverly Hills. He will also try to find out if the Bentley in the driveway in Studio City belongs to Gillete. If it does, I'll work that end. It might be a little heavy for Sadler."

"And also for a guy who drinks diet Coke. Amateurs, Jesus! Maybe you can handle one of those muscle freaks. But with Gillete and his friends you'd better carry a gun."

"When and if the time comes, I will."

He said, "I talked with a detective from LA West this morning and he reminded me of something I'd forgotten. About three years ago one of their officers blew away a drug dealer." He paused. "With a sawed-off shotgun. He had a bad record before that happened. Killing an unarmed man got him fired."

"I think I read about him—Emil something?"

"Emil Clauss. I couldn't find any address for him, but he had some drinking buddies who might know it. Denny's was one of their hangouts. We'll go there first."

Denny was alone when we entered, reading the *Racing Form.* Clauss, he told us, hadn't been in for a month and he didn't know where he lived.

"Do you know where any of his buddies live?" Lars asked.

"His best buddy lives somewhere near here, but I don't know his last name. Everybody just calls him Shorty. The boys kid him about living with some retired hooker named Big Bertha."

"I know the woman," Lars said.

"Natch," Denny said, and winked at me.

Lars glared at him.

"Let's go," I said.

A block from the tavern, Lars said, "Turn left here." A block and a half after the turn, he said, "It's that two-story house on the other side of the street."

It was a weathered frame house, painted gray, with a small front porch. There was a Room For Rent sign on one of the porch pillars.

The middle-aged woman who opened the door was tall and buxom, attired in a red-white-and-blue striped silk caftan. Her hair was henna red, her brows and lashes heavy with mascara.

"Lars!" she said. "It's been a long time, honey. What's on your mind?"

"Your friend Shorty," he said.

Her face stiffened. "Why?"

"We just want to ask him a few questions."

"About what?"

"We're trying to locate a friend of his, a man named Emil Clauss."

"That creep?" She pointed at the sign on the pillar. "It's been hanging there for three weeks now. That bastard sneaked out the night before I put it up there, owing me for board and room. He's no friend of Shorty's, not anymore."

"Do either of you know where he is now?"

She shook her head. "If you want to talk with Shorty, he's working at Avco Press in Santa Monica. Clauss used to be a cop, right?"

Lars nodded.

She looked at me. "You a cop, too?"

I shook my head.

"I didn't think so." She took a deep breath. "Clauss made us nervous all the time he was here. He's a real gun nut."

"Does that include a shotgun?"

She shrugged. "I never saw one when I made up his room." She paused to stare at Lars. "Are you talking about that man who was killed on the beach. Do you think—"

Lars lied with a shake of his head. "The man who killed him was picked up in Fresno yesterday.

But the D.A. doesn't think we have enough solid evidence to charge him."

"Ain't that always the way?" she said. "If I learn anything, Lars, I'll phone you. Who are you shacked up with now?"

"Phone me at the station," he said. *"That* number you should know by now."

As we walked to the car I asked him, "Why did you lie to her about Minatti?"

"I don't trust her. She's lied to me before. For all we know she and Clauss could be bosom buddies. If she tells Clauss about Minatti being picked up for the kill, he might figure he's in the clear."

That, I thought, was really absurd. I said nothing.

"Let's cruise around down here," he said. "In my short career at the West Side Station, I got to know some of the bad guys. Maybe we'll spot one of 'em."

Half an hour of fruitless search after that, he said, "Stop here. I think I know that guy going into the bar across the street."

It was a small corner bar next to an empty lot. The gilded letters on the front window identified it as Tessie's Tavern.

When we came in, the man who had just entered was at the far end of the bar. The woman was pouring him a glass of ale. She was tall and thin and definitely not young. Her gray-streaked hair was tied in a bun at the back. She was wearing a T-shirt and jeans. The man was dark-skinned, of medium height, maybe Hispanic, maybe not.

Lars went down to talk with him. I stayed at the near end and ordered a Miller Lite. There were only the four of us in the place.

I was halfway through my beer when the fifth character walked in—Terrible Tim Tucker.

"You lying bastard," he said. "I got the word on you!"

The three other occupants of the room were staring at us now. The woman said, "If you guys are heading for a fight, take it outside."

"We're not," I said.

"Oh, yes, we are," Tucker said, and started toward me.

"Cool it, you creep!" Lars called out, but the damned fool kept coming.

By the time I clambered off my stool, his hand was reaching for my throat. I tried to avoid his grasp, too late. I tried to kick backward into his groin, and missed.

"Damn you, stop it!" the woman shouted.

His grip tightened. Victory, if you will pardon the expression, was within his grasp. This had to be his round. My legs were turning into rubber.

But Lars was next to him now, his .38 pressed firmly against Tucker's temple. "Let go of him," Lars said, "or die where you're standing."

Tucker dropped his hands. Lars turned to face him but didn't display his shield. This was not Santa Monica. His .38 was still in his hand. "Go," he said.

Tucker looked at the gun and then at me. "We'll meet again," he said, and walked out.

Lars was smirking.

"Don't be so goddamned smug," I said. "I took him the first time."

CHAPTER SEVEN

Both the woman and the man at the far end of the bar were looking nervously at Lars. He put his gun back into his holster and smiled at both of them. "Just a little family feud," he explained.

I put a bill on the bar and we went out.

"Learn anything?" I asked him.

"Not yet. Maybe later. He's got the right connections. He's out on probation, so I'm sure he'll cooperate. He can use the Brownie points. We may as well call it a day. I can't think of any other place to go."

I took him to the Department car on the sandwich shop parking lot. "Tomorrow?" I asked.

"Only in the morning, and maybe not then. I'm way behind on my paperwork. I'll call you. If you're not at the hotel, you call me."

It was still short of four o'clock. I took the detour again, and Crystal's car was in her driveway.

She stared at me for seconds when she opened the door.

I smiled at her. "I came to apologize."

Her voice was dull. "Come in. Coffee."

"I guess. You sound gloomy."

"It's been a bad day," she said.

"Do you want to tell me about it?"

"It was only one of many," she said. "How in hell did I ever wind up in a dump like this?"

"You are still a very attractive woman, Crystal."

"Maybe for my age and weight. But Turhan is

never going to leave his old and ugly wife. He needs her money to support the cause."

"You lust for him?"

She nodded.

"He got rich in Chicago. Maybe he will again here."

She shook her head. "That life is behind him."

I considered telling her what Nolan had told me about Bay's holdings, but it could be just another of his lies. I stood up. "Are we friends again?"

She smiled and nodded and went to the door with me. She was still standing by the open doorway when I drove away.

If she had married Mike, she could have been in worse shape than she was. That damned fool! I thought back to that Saturday afternoon at Palo Alto when Cal had us down by twenty-one points at the half.

Mike had started the second half, the backup sophomore whiz kid. He had completed nineteen out of twenty-two pass attempts, including the fifty-one yarder that put us three points ahead four seconds before the final gun.

Maybe every day had to be a downer after a day like that. And today? The average salaries in the National Football League were twenty times as high as we had earned. And despite that wealth, too many of our stars were into drugs. What was it, an impulse to destroy themselves? Jocks . . .

Marijuana, Mike had insisted, was not as addictive as cigarettes and less damaging to the lungs. Mike had always believed what he needed to believe. Too many of us do.

The big surprise of today was running into Tucker at that bar. Was it only a coincidence, I wondered, or had he been tracking me? The bar was a long way from Studio City. There was a possibility that he had come down from there to visit his cousin, but I doubted it. One thing I didn't doubt was what he had promised me; we would meet again.

Dennis phoned before dinner to give me his progress report. The Bentley, he had learned, was registered by the DMV to Arnold Gillete. We had that connection now.

I told him about the incident at Tessie's Tavern and my suspicion that Tucker had been shadowing me.

"Next time you'll know," he said. "He's driving a yellow Chevrolet pickup truck." He gave me the license number.

"You must have friends at the DMV," I said.

"A brother-in-law. I have some lawyer friends, too. We need as many contacts as we can find, right?"

"Good thinking," I agreed.

"One more thing I meant to tell you. If you decide you need a gun, I have an extra one."

"Not yet."

I added this new information to the record. We had one confirmed connection now, Tucker and Gillete. Tucker and his cousin were a familial connection only, I felt. They were different breeds of cats. My record was beginning to resemble a maze.

The dinners in the hotel dining room were a little too far on the gourmet side for my peasant tastes. I walked to Heinie's for his more substantial sirloin steak and cottage fries.

Six of the booths were occupied, roughly eighty percent by males. I sat in the only vacant one.

Heinie came over to sit with me, bringing a pitcher of Einlicher with him. His wife took over the bar.

"Anything new on Mike?" he asked.

I shook my head.

"You sticking with it?"

I nodded.

"You are one stubborn Mick," he said.

"Guilty. Do you remember Terrible Tim Tucker?"

"That freak? Hell, yes! He used to drop in here once in a while when he was living in North Hollywood. He's not wrestling anymore, is he?"

"Not anymore. He's the muscle for a hoodlum named Arnold Gillete now. They live in Studio City."

Heinie tapped his forehead. "I remember now. Some reporter from the *Express* told me Tucker was connected with the mob in Chicago. That was a long time ago." He shook his head. "But Tucker isn't Italian."

"His new boss is. His real name is Arno Gilleti."

"He could be in the mob, with that name. But that Tucker freak? I can't buy it. Half the stuff the reporters feed me here is sheer bullshit. They love to pretend they have the inside story." He stood up. "Sirloin and fries?"

"Natch."

He went to the kitchen to order it. When he brought it, he went back behind the bar and his wife went home.

I played liar's poker with some of the regulars after eating and wound up fifteen dollars ahead, the best thing that had happened to me today. I was glad that Joe Nolan hadn't been in the game.

Lars had left a message for me at the hotel; he would be free to work with me tomorrow afternoon.

I wasn't looking forward to another depressing round of lies and evasions, mean streets and tawdry people. But Heinie had called it right. I was one stubborn Mick.

Lars had gone that route for decades, bringing the bad guys to justice and seeing the courts turn them free on some technicality that only a lawyer could understand.

And the ones who were convicted, like Carlos Minatti, walked out of prison long before their original termination dates on what is euphemistically called good behavior. That put them back on the streets where they could then indulge in bad behavior.

It was a restless night and a chilly and overcast morning, standard May weather for the area. Foggy in the morning, clearing by noon, except along the coast; that was the weatherman's prediction almost every May day.

I had located none of my former informants on my solo endeavor. Lars, I suspected, had run out of most of his. We could be on a dead-end road.

There was one connection I could investigate: Bay and his cousin. I phoned the temple and was told that he wouldn't be in until this afternoon.

I phoned his Brentwood home and he answered. "This is Brock Callahan," I said. "I'm sure you remember me."

"Unfortunately, I do," he said. "But Crystal has since told me you are an honorable man, except when you ply your trade. She told me you are a private investigator."

"I was, until my inheritance. I think both of us share a common goal. We want to find the person who murdered Mike Gregory. Could I come and talk with you this morning?"

"Of course."

Of course he would say "of course" was my cynical thought. I had mentioned my inheritance.

The overcast grew heavier as I drove closer to the ocean. The lannon stone home of Turhan Bay was on a wooded slope that overlooked the Brentwood Country Club.

Turhan smiled when he opened the door. He looked past me at my car on the driveway. "A sixty-five," he guessed. "A classic."

I nodded.

"I should have kept mine," he said. "Come in."

I followed him down a long hall. He led me to a small room at the end of it. There was a small desk in the room, two chairs, and a file cabinet. Two of the walls were completely shelved and jammed with books.

He sat behind the desk, I in the other chair.

"You know by now that I lied to you," I opened. "I guess it was a hangover from my previous profession. The man I really came to question you about that evening was your cousin."

"Timothy? Is he in some kind of trouble?"

"He is working for Arnold Gillete."

"I don't recognize the name. Who is he?"

"A major local hoodlum. Tim is his muscle."

He sighed. "I didn't know that. Tim and I were never very close, even in Chicago. I haven't seen or heard from him in over a year. He was quite often in trouble with the law in Chicago." He smiled. "As I was. His problems were less serious, mostly bar brawls. But you can't believe he had anything to do with Mike's death, can you? I mean—a shotgun?"

I shrugged. I said, "There's a rumor that I picked up from a friend this morning that your cousin had a Mafia connection in Chicago."

He smiled. "It's a rumor Tim circulated in Chicago, too. But it's nonsense. One of my clients was a widow who helped to pay off my detractors, and she had Italian connections, if you get what I mean. She told me Tim's rumor-mongering was the reason he had to leave Chicago."

"That makes more sense," I said.

He nodded. "I want to apologize for hiring those Arden people after your visit."

"You're forgiven," I said. "I think it would be wise if you steered clear of your cousin."

"I certainly will," he agreed.

I stood up and he walked to the door with me. He was still standing in the open doorway when I drove down his driveway to the street. If he had told the truth about his current relationship with his cousin, it bolstered my suspicion that Terrible Tim had been tailing me.

But how could I be sure? Brokers and cultists and millionaire electronic preachers—it was possible that they begin to believe their own con as their audiences grow larger and their followers more fervent. Turhan Bay, as Crystal had suggested, might really believe in his own con by now. The yippies of the sixties were the yuppies of today and money was their dream. Not all of us have rich and dead uncles.

I was relieved to see that there was no yellow Chevrolet pickup truck following me as I drove down Pico Boulevard. I turned left into Venice to learn if Denny had anything of interest to tell me.

The only thing he had to tell me was that he had heard about my fracas with Terrible Tim at Tessie's Tavern.

"Who told you about that?"

"Tessie. She's on our bartenders' bowling team. She said you were losing until Hovde took out his gun."

"I was."

"To a fucking wrestler?" He shook his head.

"Let's talk about something else."

Which we did. It was still too early to pick up Lars. We talked about the Dodgers and about the upcoming finals in the NBA between our Lakers and the Bulls.

Then, just before I left, he said, "I've been thinking about Mike. And I remembered he was the one who warned you about that guy who was out to get you. I don't mean the last one. He's dead. I mean about three years ago. What was his name?"

"Gorman," I said. "Tony Gorman."

"I remember now. If he learned that it was Mike who had alerted you, he'd have reason enough to blow Mike away, wouldn't he?"

"If he's out and around. He got a six-year sentence."

"Which means, these days, that he probably got out three years earlier than he should have."

"It certainly does. Thanks, Denny."

"You're welcome. If you go looking for him, you'd better take Hovde with you. If you can't even handle wrestlers—!"

I did not dignify his comment with a reply.

78

CHAPTER EIGHT

At the station I told Lars what Denny had reminded me about Tony Gorman.

"First things first," he said. "I think I got a hot lead on Clauss this morning."

"I was thinking maybe you could find out if Gorman is out of jail now."

"Clauss first, damn it! The hell of it is I just had orders from the Chief to stay in my own jurisdiction. The stoolie who phoned me is the man I was talking with in Tessie's Tavern. His name is Barney Luplow. I don't have his address but Tessie probably knows it."

"Okay. I'll go."

"Do that. But use some finesse for a change."

Advice on finesse from Lars? I sighed and left.

Tessie was the only occupant of the place when I entered. "Now what?" she asked.

"I came to ask if you have the address of Barney Luplow."

She studied me suspiciously. "Why? Is he in trouble?"

"Not with me. But he might have some information that I intend to pay him for. And it might keep him *out* of trouble."

She stared at me for seconds. Then: "It's about a block from here, that two-story rooming house next to the Mobil station. His room is on the second floor in back."

I left the car where it was and walked to the

place, an ancient red Victorian house, narrow-windowed, with three steps leading up to a small and sagging porch.

The door was open, the screen door closed. I went in without knocking. The stairway was on the left. There was no sound from any of the rooms as I went up the stairs. Down the narrow hall I went, past the open doorway of the bathroom to the room at the end. The door was ajar.

"Barney?" I called. "Sergeant Hovde sent me."

"Come in," a voice answered.

I pushed the door open—and saw Luplow stretched out on the floor. I heard a sound from behind the opened door, but didn't turn in time. Something heavy crashed into the back of my head and I joined Luplow on the floor. I heard the clatter of feet going down the uncarpeted stairs before the darkness arrived.

The dawn came slowly, voices first. "I know the guy," one voice said. "He's a private eye working with Lars on the Gregory kill. You remember Lars, don't you? He used to be with us."

"That was before my time," the other voice said. "Isn't he with the Santa Monica Department now?"

"Yup."

I was no longer on the floor; somebody had laid me out on the narrow bed in the room. The image of a tall, thin man began to come into focus.

"Relax," he said. "You're going to be okay. The ME assured me it was only a minor concussion."

I was in clear focus now. "Jerry Levy?" I asked.

"Right. Take it easy, Brock."

The other man was shorter, heavier, and uglier. He asked, "What in the hell were you doing here?"

Jerry said, "Don't mind my partner, Brock. He's almost as mean as Lars." He turned toward the man. "Go down and see if the landlady has come home. If she hasn't, wait there."

The man left. Jerry smiled and asked, "Now you can tell *me*. What in hell were you doing here?"

I told him the what and why and asked, "What happened to Luplow?"

"He wasn't as lucky as you were. He really got worked over. He is now at the morgue. Do you think it was Clauss who conked him?"

I shrugged. "I don't know what Clauss looks like and I never saw the man who conked me."

He smiled. "Your friend Lars is really making a crusade out of nailing Clauss, isn't he?"

"Not as much as I am. Mike Gregory was my roomie at Stanford. Are you going to take me to the West Side station?"

He shook his head. "No need. Are you going to be all right?"

I rose to a sitting position and nodded. "As soon as I can get some fresh air."

He smiled again. "Brock, next time you go out on the prowl, wear your old Rams helmet."

Or take Lars with me, I thought.

He and his partner were gone when I came down the stairs some minutes later and into the fresh air from the ocean. I walked slowly and carefully back to the car and drove to the Santa Monica station.

There the desk clerk told me Lars was out on a call and wouldn't be home until later this afternoon.

Where now? I had talked with everybody who was possibly involved, except for Arnold Gillete. That was the name I wanted to check out. I headed for Sunset Boulevard.

On my most recent visit to Los Angeles several years ago, I had come to investigate the murder of a fellow private eye, a man named Joe Puma. Joe had been the payoff man years earlier when a Mafia big shot's son had been kidnapped for ransom. The son was no longer a child when I talked with him. He had been very cooperative.

His home was a two-story brick place in Pacific Palisades, on the bluff above the Riviera Country Club. The last time I had been here there had been a 1932 Duesenberg on his guest parking area. There was none there today.

The same gray-haired, dark-skinned, middle-aged maid opened the door to my ring.

"Is Mr. Scarlatti home?" I asked. "My name is Brock Callahan."

"I remember you," she said, "and I'm sure he'll be home to you. But I had better ask him first."

A few minutes later he was at the door, a short, broad man in gray flannel slacks and a cashmere pullover.

"My favorite Ram," he said, and looked past me at the car. "When did you buy that?"

"Many years ago. I was driving a rented car last time I was here. Where's the Duesy?"

"Getting rebored. New rings, pistons, and valves, the whole bit. Come in."

We walked through an immense living room and off that to a long hall that led to his office at the rear of the house. I sat on the same chair I had sat on last time and he sat on a small couch.

"What's on your mind?" he asked.

"A man named Arnold Gillete."

"What about him?"

"Well, I had a couple of tangles with his muscle man and I don't know why. This Gillete—I wondered if he could be—you know—"

"In the Family?"

I nodded.

He smiled. "You're still skating on thin ice, aren't you?"

"Okay. I'll go quietly."

"Arnold Gillete," he said, "is not one of ours. Maybe if he gets a little richer and a little smarter, he might be some day. Who is this muscle man who's been bothering you?"

"A man named Tim Tucker, known to the video world as Terrible Tim Tucker."

"That freak? That wrestler?"

I nodded.

"He must have a death wish. Are you sure he is working for Gillete?"

"He's living with him in Studio City."

"And what do you want from me, a word of caution to Gillete?"

"No. I don't want him alerted. It's possible he had a friend of mine murdered. That's why I'm in town." I smiled. "But I wanted to make sure I wasn't getting into water over my head."

"Don't bullshit me, Brock. To use Chick Hearn's line, you'd fight King Kong on a ladder. How are Mrs. Puma and her boy doing these days?"

"Very well. She's got a good job as a legal secretary and the boy is in his second year at Cal."

He sighed. "That Joe, what a shoddy operator

he was. And you almost got yourself killed trying to find his killer. What was he to you?"

"He was one of ours," I said. "You should be able to understand that."

"Dear God!" he said. "The Sam Spade Syndrome. What was it that writer from the *Times* called you?"

"A self-anointed knight in tarnished armor." I stood up. "Thanks for what you told me."

"You're welcome. And let me know if you need any help with Gillete."

"I will," I lied.

One thing I had to admit about the Mafia, they policed their own ranks. The same could not be said about all those prestigious brokerage houses now being investigated by the Feds.

Peter Scarlatti represented the new breed in the Family tradition. The original vindictive Sicilian madmen had relied on terror. Peter's peers took a more rational businessman approach. Money was their goal, not mayhem.

If Gillete got rich enough he might be invited to join the Family. But not Terrible Tim Tucker: he was an anachronism that they could not afford. And he wasn't Italian.

I could think of no reason for Gillete to have me on his hit list. That had to be Tucker's personal vendetta. Why? Because I had questioned his cousin? If Bay had told the truth about their current relationship, that couldn't be the reason.

If, if, if . . . Somewhere in the morass of lies I had been told there had to be some seed of truth, some contradiction that would point a finger. *Patience,* I told myself.

There was a message for me at the hotel. Arnold

Gillete had phoned and asked that I phone him back any time before five o'clock.

Which I did from the room. He had just learned, he told me, about my second encounter with Tucker. He assured me it would not happen again.

"Did you find out what his beef is with me? I never met the man until I came to your house."

"And refused to tell him your name. I told him, as long as he was working for me he was on my payroll. It's possible he was trying to protect that cousin of his who runs that kooky cult in Venice. Some bartender down there told Tim that you were questioning him regarding a murder. Frankly, I didn't think the two of them were that close."

"Neither did I. Who told you about the fuss we had in Tessie's Tavern?"

"Tim did. Why do you ask?"

"Because Tessie and a police officer and the officer's informant were the only other people in the place. And the informant was killed today, murdered."

"And the police suspect Tim?"

"I have no idea. They don't confide in me."

"Well, they can't pin it on Tim. He's been here all day." He hung up.

Another lie? I had no way of knowing. But the man had no reason that I could think of to put me on his hit list. If he hoped to move up to the majors, Tim Tucker would probably have to be dumped. He was the relic of another time.

Half an hour later, Lars phoned. He said, "Jerry Levy dropped in to tell me what happened to you. You okay?"

"I'll live. Do you think the man who slugged me was Clauss?"

"I do. Levy doesn't. He thinks I'm on a crusade."

I didn't comment.

"About tomorrow, Brock. I got a lot of static about my piled-up paperwork when I came back to the station and a few nasty remarks about jurisdiction. I'll call you when the paperwork is cleared up."

"Okay. Good luck. Keep the faith."

My head was aching. I took a couple of aspirins and a long, warm shower, trying to wash away the frustrations of this day. Mike was dead. Finding his killer wouldn't bring him back. How long could I stay on the hunt?

The combined efforts of Callahan, Hovde, Sadler, and the Santa Monica Police Department had come up with nothing. Lars was back to his paperwork; the SMPD must have decided by now that they had spent too much time on a low priority case, a dead pigeon.

Sadler phoned before dinner to tell me that he, too, had come up with nothing of substance. And, he added, his wife had decided that not *all* of his vacation time should be spent in sleuthing. They were going to Palm Springs for the weekend. Was that okay with me?

I assured him that it was and I might go home myself.

"You're not quitting."

"Not yet."

Lars had probably not checked out the present whereabouts of Tony Gorman. I didn't phone him to ask if he had; Clauss was his current obsession.

Heinie was familiar with that case. Heinie was familiar with all of the major cases I had worked down here. And it had been twenty-four hours since I had feasted on his sirloin steak and cottage fries.

There were only four booths occupied when I entered. Jose was behind the bar. Heinie was sitting with a couple of sports writers from the local papers.

He left them and went to get a pitcher of Einlicher to bring to my booth. "Your usual?" he asked.

I nodded. He went to the kitchen to order it. When he came back to sit across from me, I asked him, "Do you remember Tony Gorman?"

"I do." He frowned. "You're not thinking that he might be the guy who aced Mike?"

"He could be. Do you know where he is now?"

He shook his head. "He must still be in the slammer. Didn't he get six years?"

"Three years ago."

"I see what you mean. I'll ask around. That was a Beverly Hills pinch, wasn't it?"

"It was. You've got an in there, haven't you?"

"Only with the day watch," he said. "I'll go there tomorrow."

I ate and we yacked about this and that, none of it worth recording, and then I left. The boys at the bar were already into their game of liar's poker. By leaving now I would still be ahead from last night.

CHAPTER NINE

Heinie phoned in the morning to tell me Gorman had been released from prison two weeks ago and was now living at a halfway house in the San Fernando Valley. The name of the place was Second Chance. He gave me the address.

There had been certain discrepancies in Gorman's trial that had troubled me at the time. Mike had told me Gorman was a dealer. I had investigated and found out it was true. It was when Gorman was out on bail that Mike had warned me about the vendetta. But the history of the man, according to the Beverly Hills police, had never included any acts of violence.

The day was again overcast when I left the hotel. The sun was out in the Valley. The place called Second Chance was a long, narrow, gray wooden building in Tarzana. It looked like it had once been an army barracks.

There was no doorbell; I went in. There were several steel chairs in this small room and a desk next to the open doorway that led to the hall. A heavyset man in faded jeans and a tan T-shirt was sitting behind the desk. The man standing in front of it turned as I closed the door.

It was Gorman. He was thinner and his hair a shade grayer. He smiled.

"I figured you'd show up here," he said. "It's about Mike, isn't it? I read about it in the paper. Were you the man who phoned?"

I shook my head. "Could we talk?"

"Why not?" he said. "This way."

He led me down a long hall past a string of closed doors to an open door at the end. There was a small bureau in this room, an army cot, two wooden kitchen chairs, and a draped area against one wall that probably served as a clothes closet.

He sighed. "It's a long way from Beverly Hills, isn't it? Sit down and tell me why you're here. If you want to know where I was the night Mike died, you can ask the man at the desk. He runs this place."

"That's not the reason I'm here, Tony." I sat down on one of the chairs, he on the cot. "I've been thinking about the trial."

"You're thinking I might have got jobbed?"

I nodded.

"Callahan, I *never* put anybody on the stuff. I had the Beverly Hills trade and the studio trade, sniffers, all of 'em. That was enough for me; I'm not that greedy. They all paid up front. But Mike, ugh!"

"What about him?"

"He was into me for over two grand. And when I pressed him, he finked to you. My only charity case —and he finks!" He took a deep breath. "I liked the guy! Nobody else ever got into me for that kind of money."

I said, "I had no idea Mike was into the heavy stuff. Marijuana, I knew about that. He was smoking that when we were roomies."

"That damned fool," he said. "The golden boy! The way I see it, he killed himself."

I said nothing.

"Any other favorite suspect?" he asked.

"A man named Clauss."

"Emil Clauss?"

I nodded. "Do you know the man?"

"All my brethren know him," he said. "A vicious cop and on the take. But he never bothered me. The small dealers were his bread and butter. Beverly Hills was not on his beat."

"The search is out for him, Tony. Maybe you have friends who can help us."

"I've never been a stoolie," he said, "but maybe in this case. A crooked cop who blew away an unarmed dealer? I could switch. I'll ask around. Leave me your phone number."

"I'm staying at the Beverly Hills Hotel."

"So was I," he said sadly. "For years. And now this!"

I couldn't see Gorman as a killer. Asking the man at the desk for Tony's alibi would be ungracious. I didn't need to. He informed me that Tony had been sound asleep the night Mike was killed.

I drove out of the Valley sun and headed back down toward foggy Santa Monica. Clauss had probably killed that unarmed drug dealer because he didn't pay off. It had lost him his job and turned him more vicious than ever. Both Denny and Heinie had confirmed that Mike was far from solvent; he couldn't even pay his bar tabs. That would be pickings too small to interest Clauss. But Clauss was not a rational man.

Crystal was out in front, clipping her solitary rosebush. "Now what?" she asked.

"I thought maybe I could take you to some expensive place for lunch."

"Are you coming on to me?"

"Nope. Just a friendly visit to an old friend."

"You could have dropped the 'old.' I have to be back here at two-thirty. Turhan's coming then."

"For an afternoon quickie?"

She glared at me. "For our meditation session, you foul-minded jock! Turhan has helped me through some bad times, just as he tried to do for Mike. You can leave now."

"I apologize, Crystal. Please?"

"Okay, okay! Maybe you had a right. I'll admit I've never been the village virgin. I'll have to change. You can watch a game show on the tube. That should fit your mentality."

"I love 'em," I lied.

She was wearing a blue silk sheath and blue pumps when she came out again, a welcome change from today's silly fashions.

In the car, she said, "Do you remember when you asked me if I lusted for Turhan and I said I did?"

"Yes."

"I lied. He's gay."

"And married—?"

"His wife's a lesbian."

"Let's hope his devoted followers never learn that. I'm almost beginning to believe he means what he says, even if I don't understand it."

"It's kind of complicated. He has this belief that ours can't possibly be the only planet in the universe. That would be sheer arrogance. There must be thousands of inhabited planets out there somewhere. And a lot of them with a more advanced civilization."

"I sure as hell hope so," I said. "I ain't too crazy about this one."

The sun came out. The food was fine, though

not exactly geared to my peasant palate. We talked of other times and old friends, and where were they all today? As some sage has said, nostalgia ain't what it used to be.

I took her home in time for her celestial seance and drove to Denny's.

The bar was lined with males, except at the far end where Denny was paying off a female winner.

She left with a handful of twenties and I took her place at the bar.

"Did you get a chance to check out Gorman?" he asked.

I nodded. "He's clean."

"Clean? A drug pusher, clean? What kind of talk is that?"

"He wasn't a pusher; only a dealer. And he confined his trade to rich suckers."

"That's better, but still not clean. Anything new on the murder?"

I shook my head. He set a glass of Einlicher in front of me. I asked, "Did you ever pay off Clauss?"

"Never! For my puny take? And a lot of my customers are mean and tough and they don't like crooked cops."

He went down to the other end to serve a customer. The place was getting noisy and crowded, I finished my beer and left.

Gorman had been cleared. So had Carlo Minatti. That left us Clauss as our prime suspect.

The longest line of connections on my sheet was Gillete, Tucker, Bay, and Nolan. If Clauss was the who, what was the why? Motive, means, and opportunity are the deadly triplicate that a prosecutor requires for a Murder One conviction. What was the motive?

I'd had almost a week of frustration, leading nowhere. My image of Mike had deteriorated in that time. Peter Scarlatti was probably right; I was a victim of the Sam Spade syndrome. Mike was my Archer. Archer had been Spade's partner; Mike had been my roomie.

Denny had not paid off Clauss. But Denny, so far as I knew, did not deal in drugs. Gorman had told me the small dealers were Clauss's bread and butter. That description would include Mike. It wasn't likely that he would get the Beverly Hills trade.

Did he, I wondered, know that Turhan Bay was homosexual? If he did, it would be a motive for blackmail. That, I decided, was taking my image of Mike to a new low. And the possibility of Bay hiring a vicious killer like Clauss was highly unlikely.

It was possible that if we ever found Clauss, we would have the who. But we wouldn't have the why. To paraphrase Sherwood Anderson, I wanted to know why. What was Emil's motive?

The bullet from a pistol or rifle can be matched to the gun. But not a shotgun. Clauss obviously knew that. It could be the reason the shotgun was his choice.

CHAPTER TEN

Gorman phoned in the morning to tell me that all he had learned about Clauss so far was that he had a son named Emil. The word he had on him was that they had never got along since Clauss's wife had divorced him.

"Is she still in town?"

"No. She moved to Bakersfield right after the divorce."

"No other children?"

"None. And there's no listing for young Clauss in the phone book. The only other word I got was from a doubtful source. I was told he used to live in the Brentwood area. At that time he was driving a red Porsche with wire wheels."

Clauss, who couldn't pay his rent, had a son who lived in Brentwood and drove a Porsche. I could understand why young Emil had no listing in the phone book.

I ate breakfast at the hotel and came out into a sunny day for a Sunday tour of Brentwood. Back and forth I drove, on the main streets and the lateral streets, hoping against hope I would spot a red Porsche with wire wheels.

On one of the lateral streets off Wilshire, about three blocks from Bay's house, my luck held. A car of that description was parked in front of a two-story stucco apartment house.

There were five names on the mailboxes in the vestibule. There was one blank space. I pressed the button next to that one. There was no answering buzz on the locked door nor any answer on the vestibule phone.

I went out to sit in the car. I sat and sat and sat and wished I hadn't given up smoking.

A few minutes before I had decided to leave, a stocky young man in tennis shorts and carrying a racquet came out of the building and headed for the Porsche.

I walked across the street as he was about to get into the car. "Are you Emil Clauss?" I asked.

He nodded and smiled. "And I know who you are. I grew up watching you perform at the Coliseum. Are you the man who rang my bell?"

I nodded.

"If I had known it was you, I would have answered. But too damned many cops have been ringing my bell lately."

"Looking for your father?"

"Right." He frowned. "Wait—didn't you work as a private detective after you left the Rams?"

"I did. I'm retired now. I live in San Valdesto. But a very good friend of mine was killed and I came down to investigate it."

"And that's why you're looking for my father. He could have done it. Jesus, he put my mother into intensive care."

"So far," I said, "he is only a suspect. We have to remember he could be innocent."

"Not of beating up my mother. The last I heard about him, he was boarding in some house in Venice with a former hooker."

"He's left there. And stiffed the lady for room and board. If you get any information on him, please phone the police."

96

"No way! I've had a belly full of cops. I'll phone you. This friend you mentioned, was that Mike Gregory?"

I nodded.

"That damned fool."

"Did you know him?"

"No, but I watched him on the tube that day he beat Cal. And he winds up a dead derelict on the beach. What a waste!"

"Drugs," I said.

He nodded. "Drugs and dumb jocks. But not in tennis, not yet."

"Not yet," I said, and told him where I was staying.

Clauss, so far, was only a suspect. We were running out of those. Gorman's innocence had been certified. The Fresno police had established Carlo Minatti's. If Clauss made that an unholy trinity, we were out of suspects, the end of the road.

There were old friends in town I probably should have visited, but I had been in the car too long. Crystal was the closest.

She was out on her small front lawn, in shorts and halter, digging up dandelions.

She stood up and stared at me. "Twice in two days? I'm beginning to think you've got the hots for me."

"Not in any vulgar way. I am only a worn-out traveler seeking pleasant company."

"The Sunday blues," she said. "I get 'em, too. Maybe we should go to church."

"I'd prefer the beach."

"So would I," she said. "We can walk there from here. I could use the exercise."

"Let's go."

She packed a lunch, including four bottles of beer. An old blanket and a large parasol made up the rest of our luggage.

The beach was jammed. We walked to the far end, to a more sparsely populated area and set up the parasol and spread the blanket and sat down to watch the waves come in. It was nirvana time, a haven from the external realities.

"That friend of yours, that Lars," she said. "How can you stand him? He's a slob."

"Because he busted you?"

"And propositioned me. It would be like being run over by a truck. He's so big and gross."

"Lars propositioned you?"

"He did. Don't you dare mention it to him!"

"I won't. I know he's a horny guy. But he is also an officer of the law. Why didn't you report him to his superiors?"

"And have him put me on his enemy list? No, thanks."

I said, "Lars isn't as big and gross as Terrible Tim Tucker. Did you ever meet him?"

"Turhan's cousin? A long time ago. Turhan looked him up when he first came out here. I guess they didn't hit it off. Isn't he a boxer?"

"A former wrestler, now a bodyguard for a local hoodlum."

She looked at me suspiciously. "Are you interrogating me? Are you suggesting that Turhan might have something to do with Mike's murder?"

"Of course not! Don't be so damned suspicious. I'm your friend, Crystal. Let's go wading."

I took off my shoes and socks, she her sandals, and we splashed along in the shallow water all the way to Muscle Beach. I was more bushed than she was when we got back. Which she pointed out.

I tried to think of some acerbic comment to make about that. None came to mind.

We ate the sandwiches and drank the beer and watched the waves roll in, the swimmers and the waders and the young splashers, back again to nirvana time.

When we got up to go, I suggested that maybe a dinner and a movie might be a pleasant way to end the day.

She shook her head. "Some other time. Turhan is giving a talk tonight on world peace. Maybe you'd like to come with me?"

"Not tonight."

We walked back to her house in silence. I had the feeling she was miffed. Before I got back into the car I asked her if she was.

She sighed. "Nostalgic, I guess. Were things really better when we were younger or is that only what I want to believe?"

I shrugged. "I don't know. If I had my druthers, I wouldn't mind being young again."

"You weren't rich then."

"But I was handsomer."

She kissed me. "You're handsome enough for me. If your wife ever divorces you, put me on top of your substitution list. Thanks for today, Brock."

"And thank you. Any time you have need of me, holler."

She smiled. "I will. You're not nearly as heavy as Lars."

"You are a vulgar woman, Crystal Lane."

"I know."

"What a waste" young Clauss had said about Mike. The same could apply to Crystal. Pretty and smart and stylish, a victim of unsuitable suitors. It would be unfair to accuse her of having a love of money, the core of all evil. She didn't love money, only the spending of it.

I was having my predinner drink in the dining room when Joe Nolan walked in. He saw me and came over.

"May I join you?" he asked. "My wife is out of town, visiting relatives."

"So is mine. Be my guest."

He shook his head. "This one's on me again. I can pretend you're a client and put it on my expense account."

The waiter came. He ordered mineral water. He sighed. "I thought I didn't need AA but I was wrong. Is there anything new on Mike's murder?"

"Nothing. I have a feeling I am going down a dead-end road. And the Santa Monica police seem to have dropped it from a low priority case to a no priority case."

"How about that Gillete person you mentioned. Isn't he a suspect?"

"Not to the Santa Monica boys. But, of course, he is out of their jurisdiction."

"And Turhan? You don't think he was involved in any way?"

"Not so far."

He smiled again. "I'll bet you think that blackmail theory of mine was dumb. My wife claims I read too many mystery novels."

"It wasn't dumb, now that I've learned more about Mike. I still hope to do a little more digging

100

on Bay. But that could cost you a wealthy client, couldn't it?"

He shook his head. "Not really. If he goes to jail the account would still be mine."

I frowned.

"That was cynical, wasn't it?" he asked. "My wife also claims I have a macabre sense of humor."

"I agree with your wife," I told him.

He left before our dessert arrived. He explained that he had a ticket for a Springsteen concert.

He went to the concert. I went up to my room. What had I learned today? I had learned that young Clauss hated his father, Turhan Bay was lecturing on world peace tonight, and Nolan was back in AA. I consoled myself with the thought that Sunday was not supposed to be a working day.

Lars had settled on Clauss as his target. But all of them—Nolan, Bay, Crystal, Gillete, and Tucker —could be involved, one way or another, with the death of Mike Gregory.

Clauss was the logical choice at the moment. But how were the others involved? Tucker could be a logical suspect, or any hit man Gillete could hire.

It might have been Clauss who had conked me in that rooming house. My choice would be Tucker. Tucker was the muscle man. Luplow hadn't been shot; he had been beaten to death.

There was, of course, a possibility it was both the muscle and the hit man. He was mean enough. And the sound of a shot in that second-story room was bound to alert the tenants. If there had been any roomers on the first floor, they could have identified the killer when he came clattering down the stairs.

The noise of a rumpus on the floor above would

probably sound to them like just another family dispute.

There were too many "ifs" and too many "maybes" in this case. It was after midnight when I finally fell asleep.

CHAPTER ELEVEN

The morning *Times* reported that the man who had killed Barney Luplow was now in jail. Lars would not learn from Luplow where Clauss was hiding.

I thought of phoning him to tell him what young Clauss had told me yesterday, but decided not to. I was still angry about what Crystal had told me. Lars claimed he hated crooked cops. Sexual favors, apparently, did not qualify as extortion to a fornicator.

I phoned Dennis Sadler and suggested we ride together today.

"Okay," he said. "I'll pick you up at the hotel in an hour."

I had finished breakfast and was out in front of the hotel when he drove up the driveway in a dark-yellow Chevrolet two-door sedan. The town was loaded with that model. It was the kind of inconspicuous car the smart investigators favored for shadowing or surveillance.

"How was Palm Springs?" I asked.

"Perfect! Domestic harmony has returned to our house."

"And your mother-in-law?"

"Hopeless. Where first?"

"The Valley. Studio City."

Traffic heading into downtown Los Angeles was heavy. It was light on our trip to the Valley. The

Bentley and the yellow pickup truck were parked in front of the Gillete garage.

We drove past, made a U-turn at the nearest intersection, and parked on the far side of the road across from the house. We had a clear view of it from here, parked behind a hedge.

Dennis asked, "What makes you think Gillete could be involved in your friend's murder?"

"Tim Tucker, Bay's cousin. I met him first when I came here to check on Bay. But the second time I ran into him was in a small bar in Venice, a long way from here. I don't know if he was looking for me or if it was only a coincidence. My guess is that he followed me. Then Gillete phoned me to apologize for the fuss Tim and I had at the bar. I wondered why."

"Maybe Tucker followed you on his own because he learned you were investigating his cousin."

I shook my head. "They're not that close."

"That's a doubtful confirmation, Brock."

"Probably. But what else do we have? I've been lucky before, working on instinct."

"So have I," he said.

He reached into the backseat and picked up a pair of binoculars. He took a notebook and a ball-point pen out of his jacket pocket and handed them to me.

"We don't need the binoculars," I said. "We can see from here what's going on down there."

"But not the license plates of any visitors," he explained.

It had been a long time since I had done any surveillance. I said nothing.

We sat. There was no radio in the car. We sat in silence.

About twenty minutes later he said, "That cop who came with you when you came to our office, that Hovde, he's a real cowboy, isn't he."

"Yup."

"The boss thinks he's on the take."

"Your boss is wrong. Lars hates crooked cops. And your boss is also dumb if he supports Turhan Bay."

"I know. I wish he was half as generous with his help as he is with that faker."

More silence.

Two cars came down the hill in the next fifteen minutes; none came up. When one finally did, a jet-black Cadillac, we missed the reading on the front plate. We hadn't known it was going to turn into the driveway; no signal light had shown.

"We'll get the back-plate number when it leaves," Dennis said.

The minutes dragged on. The car got hotter. "We should have brought a six-pack," I said.

"There's a bottle of spring water behind your seat," he told me.

It was a vacuum bottle and the water was cool. We sat.

The Cad finally left and he read me the plate, which I recorded. A few minutes after that, Terrible Tim came out and raised the hood of his truck.

Several more cars went down the hill, one came up. Tim closed the hood of his truck and went into the house. It was close to noon now and the car was an oven.

I could be home, swimming in the pool, I could be playing golf. Was Mike worth all this? The Mike who had been my roomie, yes. But now? What was

I, the avenger? Somebody had to be, I told myself. Who else gives a damn? Certainly not the SMPD.

Tucker came out of the house and climbed into the truck.

"Should we follow him?" Dennis asked.

I nodded. "Let's hope he's heading for the ocean. It should be a lot cooler down there."

He was. Traffic was heavy on Ventura Boulevard; we stayed close to the truck. Dennis dropped back as the traffic thinned.

"You're good at this," I said.

"I always thought I was. But my mother-in-law won't even ride with us unless my wife drives."

Down the pass, toward the ocean. The ocean breeze hit us about halfway down. He adjusted our pace to the flow of traffic, staying out of sight. The truck turned left on Olympic, into Venice. The traffic was minimal here; we stayed far behind.

The For Rent sign was still on Big Bertha's boardinghouse pillar when we drove by. A block and a half later, Tucker turned into an alley.

"That's a dead-end alley," Dennis said. "Let's get out."

Tucker was walking toward a deserted one-story cement block building when we came to the mouth of the alley. The building was at the far end.

When he went in we went partway down and crouched behind a huge dumpster, out of sight.

A few minutes later he came out carrying a large cardboard box. He put it into the bed of the truck. He went back in and came out again moments later carrying a suitcase. He put that next to the box and turned to look back at the building.

About a minute later, a bulky bald man with

snow-white eyebrows came out of the building, carrying another, smaller, suitcase.

The truck backed out of the alley. When we came out to the street it was nowhere in sight.

"They're probably heading back to Gillete's house," Dennis said.

"Probably. Do you know where Ye Sandwiche Shoppe is."

He nodded.

"Drive there."

"Why?"

"Hovde might be there. I want a read on that bald guy."

Lars was there, sitting with a uniformed officer. I related the events of the morning to him and finished by describing the bald man with the white eyebrows and our guess as to where he was heading.

"Clauss," he said. The uniformed man nodded agreement.

"I'll alert the Valley boys," Lars said. He left the booth.

The uniformed man looked at Dennis. "Don't you work for Arden?"

Dennis nodded.

The man's smile was scornful. He looked at me. "You another private eye?"

I shook my head. "I'm the Chief of Police in Yuba City. What's it to you?"

He stared at me and I at him. Dennis smiled and yawned.

When Lars came back he told us the Valley cops were sending a car to watch the house. "I should hear from them in about half an hour. Sit down and have a cup of coffee while we wait."

"We're going to have lunch here," I told him. "We'll find another booth."

He stared at me. "You sore about something?"

"The company you keep."

In our booth, Dennis said, "I thought you and Hovde were buddies."

"No comment."

"I was thinking," he said, "maybe Tucker didn't take Clauss to Gillete's house. Maybe he took him to his cousin's house."

"I doubt it. You really hate Bay, don't you?"

"Yes. I hate all those blood-sucking electronic preachers, too."

When we finished our lunch I asked him, "Do you think your friend at DMV would tell you the name of the owner of that Cadillac we saw at Gillete's house?"

He nodded and got up to use the pay phone next to the kitchen door. Several minutes later he came back to tell me that the owner of the Cadillac was a man named Winthrop Loeb.

"That name rings a bell," he said. "Do you recognize it?"

"I do. He's an attorney. He defended some pretty hairy characters and got them off. That includes a couple of major mob big shots."

He took a breath. "That's too heavy for me."

"And me," I agreed. "What we need now is finesse. I'll check out the man."

"Where? How?"

"Through a friend who should know."

He stared at me. "If you're thinking what I'm suspecting, please don't mention my name to your friend."

"I won't. There is one more place Clauss could

have gone to, but it's a doubtful one. His son lives in Brentwood. He might be home."

I directed him to the apartment house and went in to ring young Clauss's bell. Nothing.

When I came out to the car, Dennis asked, "Now where?"

"Back to the hotel for me. I'm beginning to stink. I need a shower. I'll phone my friend from there."

He asked, "Should I come back here tonight and watch the place?

I shook my head. "Young Emil promised me that I would be the first to know if his father ever showed up here. He really hates the man."

He drove me back to the hotel. There were no messages for me. I took a shower before I phoned the Peter Scarlatti residence.

He answered the phone. I told him about Loeb's visit to Gillete's house.

"So what?" he asked.

"Well, as you warned me, I shouldn't skate on thin ice."

"Ain't you the cute one? The ice is a little thicker this time. Winthrop is no longer involved in criminal defense cases. Financial manipulations are his current interest. *He* is now the man who is skating on thin ice. But not with us, with the Feds."

"Thank you, sir."

"You're welcome. Next time you plan to go up against Terrible Tim Tucker, let me know. That one I want to see."

"I'll be sure to send you a free ticket," I said.

I added what I had learned today into the record and searched one more time for the pointing finger. *Nada.* I was putting the sheets back into the folder when the phone rang.

The desk clerk told me there was a man in the lobby named Lars Hovde who wished to speak to me. Should he send him up?

I said he could.

Lars was scowling when I opened the door. "That smartass clerk downstairs made me show him my shield."

I shrugged. "Come in."

He came in. "What's your beef with me?" he asked. "You were really snotty at the restaurant."

"It's been a bad day, Lars. And I've been a little resentful about the lack of interest the Santa Monica Department is showing in Mike's death."

"Jesus! I've been trying to hunt down Clauss every free minute I've had."

"Clauss, yes. Because you hate crooked cops and Clauss is one of them."

"What are you, a mind reader? Cut out the bullshit, Brock."

I put a hand on his shoulder. "Let's drop the subject. Let's go down to the bar and I'll buy you a drink."

"Okay. But next time you have a beef with me, speak up. I've got a hunch that your friend Crystal has told you some lies about me."

"That's crazy," I said. "Let's go."

Two drinks and some small talk later he left, promising that he would work with me again as soon as he could find the time.

Maybe, just maybe, Crystal had lied to me about him.

CHAPTER TWELVE

A coincidence I had overlooked came to mind as I was having dinner. The same day I had returned to the hotel after questioning Peter Scarlatti about Gillete, Gillete had phoned me. Maybe it wasn't a coincidence. Had Peter phoned Gillete after I left? I hoped that if he had, he said some kind things about me, such as Peter being a very good friend of mine.

So many lies had been told, so many false trails followed . . . I had told a few lies myself, but only, I assured myself, in the cause of justice.

It was a balmy evening, too pleasant to spend indoors with the boob tube. Lars and I had not talked with Big Bertha's Shorty when we had visited her. He had been at work. I drove there.

Bertha was wearing a green-and-black striped caftan tonight, her brows and lashes devoid of mascara.

"You again!" she said. "Now what?"

"I was wondering if I could talk with Shorty."

"Why?"

"Because I'm still looking for Clauss."

"You got a name?"

"Brock Callahan."

"Wait here," she said.

A minute later a short and chunky man with a crew cut was at the door. He stared at me. "By God, it is! I thought Bertha was kidding me. Come in, come in."

I came into a hall with a staircase on the right-hand side and an archway to a small living room on the left. The room was furnished in old-fashioned and heavy pieces of dark mahogany chairs and a davenport upholstered in brown velour, all of them with carved arms.

"Sit down," he said. "Want a beer?"

I sat in one of the chairs. "No, thanks. I had two drinks before dinner."

He sighed. "Well, I guess I can live without one for a while." He sat down in the upholstered chair across from me. "Nothing new on Clauss, huh?"

"Nothing." I told him about my talk with young Clauss, our identification of him in Venice and how we had lost track of him. "I wondered if you might know of any place where he could be hiding?"

He shook his head. "That bastard! Bertha told me about your visit, but she only mentioned Lars. She's not a sports fan. And she didn't know Emil had *two* shotguns. One of 'em is a short-barrel twelve-gauge blaster. You know, the man was almost human before he started having trouble with his wife. He thought she was cheating on him because he wasn't getting any nooky from her. Who can blame her, huh? He ain't no Robert Redford."

"Do you think she was cheating on him?"

"No way! She's a real religious woman. She moved to Bakersfield after the divorce. She didn't get one dime in alimony."

"Do you think Clauss is still in town?"

"Probably. Hell, he grew up here. He went to school in Santa Monica from kindergarten on." He paused. "And he's got buddies who won't fink on him. That's why I told Bertha not to get too nosy."

"I can guess that you feel the same way."

112

He nodded. "But if I learn anything without asking around, I'll phone you. I mean, if you plan to stay in town."

"I do. You don't want to call Lars?"

He shook his head. "I'll call you. Where are you staying?"

"At the Beverly Hills Hotel." I stood up. "Thanks for what you told me. I appreciate it."

He smiled. "Would you do me one favor?"

"Name it."

He got up and left the room. He came back with a well-worn, slightly lopsided football and a ball-point pen filled with white ink. He handed both to me.

"What's your full name?" I asked.

"Bolger," he said. "Make it to Shorty Bolger."

Which I did, the high point of my day.

From there I drove past Tessie's Tavern on the off chance there might be a yellow pickup truck parked near it. There wasn't. And there were no lights on in Turhan's temple. I drove to Brentwood, planning to tell young Emil about tailing his father this morning and to warn him that he might still be in this area.

There was no red Porsche in front of the building and no answer to my ring. I went back to the hotel.

My file was getting thicker, but no clearer. I went to bed and had a weird dream. Jan and Crystal were both sitting with me on the beach and quarreling. And both of them were naked.

The radio had the standard weather report in the morning; foggy in the morning, clearing by noon, except along the coast. It was probably a taped message. It was misty in Beverly Hills.

The fulcrum in this seesaw choice of suspects was Tucker. He was Bay's cousin; he was the muscle man and errand boy for Gillete. Our prime choice for the *who* was now Clauss. But what was the *why?*

I voiced these thoughts to Dennis when he phoned before breakfast. He agreed with me that finding Tucker was our best choice for success.

When he picked me up, I told him where I had been last night and what I had learned.

"If Clauss is still in that end of town," he said, "he might find out where his son lives."

"He hasn't up to now. And if he had learned it earlier he stayed away."

"He hasn't been a hunted man until now."

"That's true," I admitted.

"I think," he said, "that we should find out where young Clauss works and warn him. Did you learn that when you talked with him?"

I shook my head. "That was dumb of me. And I didn't get his unlisted phone number. I could have phoned him this morning."

He said nothing; he was a polite young man.

Neither the Bentley nor the truck were visible when we drove past Gillete's house. But the garage door was closed. Both of them could be in there.

We sat. At twenty dollars an hour for him and zilch for me, we sat. Traffic on the street was heavier today, the weather comfortably cooler. Most of the traffic was going downhill and most of the drivers were women. The Broadway Department Store was having its semiannual storewide sale.

A few minutes later the garage door opened and a man in coveralls came out, carrying clippers and

114

a rake. The Bentley was in the garage, but not the truck.

"Damn it!" Dennis said. "Now where?"

I shrugged. "Back to where the action is, I suppose."

Back to the sea. We prowled through Venice and Santa Monica, then stopped in Brentwood, hoping that young Clauss was home, so we could warn him. He wasn't.

"As long as we're here," I said. "Let's check out Bay. His place is only a few blocks from here."

The thought was good; our luck was bad. The yellow truck was coming toward us on the other side of the street when we were almost a block from Bay's house. Cars were parked on both sides of the street. Dennis gunned the car, made a screeching U-turn at the next corner, and headed back.

The yellow truck was nowhere in sight on any of the streets we passed nor the street we were on.

"That bastard!" he said.

"Back to Bay's house," I said.

I went to the house and Dennis stayed in the car when we got back there.

Bay looked troubled when he came to the door. I asked him, "Was your cousin just here?"

He nodded. "He just left," he said wearily, "two thousand dollars richer than when he came."

"Blackmail?" I asked.

He nodded. "He threatened to tell my followers about something that could lose me my ministry."

"Your Chicago history?"

He nodded again. "And some other things he knew about me which I do not care to discuss. He told me he had lost his job and needed the money.

He was here for two hours. I had to wait for the bank to open. He wanted cash. He claimed he had to get out of town. I'm sure he lied about that."

"Maybe not. His former boss is a hoodlum and it's possible Tim did something the man didn't approve of."

"I hope so."

"If he comes back again," I said, "call the police. He's involved with a man named Emil Clauss, a former cop who is suspected of Mike Gregory's murder. Clauss worked at the West Side station before he was fired."

"One of my people is a detective there," he told me. "I'll phone him."

When I came back to the car, Dennis asked, "Anything?"

"Blackmail," I said.

I didn't tell him about the "other things" Bay had alluded to. I could guess what they were. That would be his secret. Revealing it would bring me down to the Tim Tucker level.

He asked, "Do you think Tucker was lying about having to leave town?"

"Maybe. I wonder if the Valley cops questioned him after Lars alerted them?"

"Lars would know," he said.

"Let's prowl for a while," I said.

He smiled. "Still on the outs with your buddy?"

"No comment."

We drove back to the warehouse where Clauss had been holed up, to see if had left anything incriminating there. The odor that assailed us as we entered was not foreign to me. It was the same as the odor from our septic tank when the winter rains caused it to overflow.

116

The water had apparently been turned off when the building was deserted. There was a concrete pit in one corner that could have been used for oil drains if this had once been a garage. It was now serving as a toilet.

We found nothing that would help us in our short search before the odor drove us out.

In the car again, I told Dennis what Peter Scarlatti had told me about attorney Winthrop Loeb.

"Do you think Gillete has a Mafia connection?" he asked.

"Not yet. But that could be why he dumped Tucker. Tucker wouldn't be an asset to the mob, not these days."

He shook his head. "Clauss and Tucker I might be able to handle. But I don't want to tangle with the big boys."

"We might not have to. Loeb is now being investigated by the Feds. That could include Gillete if they're working together."

We stayed in the Venice and Santa Monica area, from the mean streets to the better ones and down all the alleys. The day was getting warmer and the car hotter.

We were close to desperation time when we spotted the yellow pickup truck in the poorer section of Santa Monica. When we got closer we could read the license number. It was Tucker's truck.

It was parked on a pitted blacktop driveway in front of an ancient frame house badly in need of paint. A sign on the parched front lawn stated that the place was available for sale or rent.

"I'll take the front door," I said. "If the place has a back door, you can watch that."

He studied me doubtfully for seconds before he nodded.

There were two low and worn steps in front of the doorway. The door was ajar. There was no sound from inside. I pushed the door open a few more inches. The floor was uncarpeted in this, the probable living room. The air was musty. The window in the right-hand wall, which I could see, was almost opaque with dust.

I stepped in. The only furniture in the room was an old mission oak sideboard, topped with a cracked mirror. The kitchen sink was visible through the opened doorway at the far end of the room. There was another doorway in the wall to the left.

There was still no sign or sound of life. I moved along the left wall and peered in.

It was a small room. There was an open sleeping bag on the floor in the center of the room and two unopened suitcases next to the far wall. Tim Tucker was lying on the floor in the center of the room, next to the sleeping bag. His eyes were open, but he wasn't seeing anything.

I went out and through the kitchen to the back door. Dennis was standing next to a tall eucalyptus tree. "Get to a phone as quick as you can and call the police. Tucker is in here. He's dead."

CHAPTER THIRTEEN

Dennis and I were sitting in Lieutenant Slade's office when a uniformed officer came in to tell him there was no identification on Tucker, no driver's license, no credit cards, no wallet, nothing. The cause of death appeared to be poison but the medical examiner had not confirmed it yet. The officers had found an almost-empty pint bottle of whiskey in the room. It was being analyzed now.

Slade said, "We already have identification. Let me know as soon as you have confirmation."

The officer nodded and left. Slade looked at me. "Sergeant Hovde told me you and Tucker had a fracas at some bar in Venice."

"We did. Lars was with me when it happened. We were working together. Did he tell you that?"

"Don't be insolent, Mr. Callahan."

"I won't if you won't. We phoned you to report a murder, not to confess. I hope you are giving this murder more attention than you did Mike Gregory's."

He glared at me and turned to Dennis. "You work for Arden, don't you?"

Dennis nodded.

"We don't always get full cooperation from your office."

Dennis nodded again. "My boss has this strange theory that cooperation should be a two-way street."

Silence in the room.

I asked, "May I phone my attorney now?"

"Why?"

"So we can get the hell out of here."

"You're not being held and you're not being charged. I assumed you'd want to wait for the report on the poison."

The uniformed man came in before I could answer. The whiskey, he told Slade, had been analyzed. It had been laced with arsenic.

When he left, Slade said, "Okay, you two can go now. But stay available."

Outside, Dennis said, "No wallet? Does that mean no two thousand dollars? I'll bet both of the cops who showed up are richer than they were when they got there."

"Easy, Dennis! The guy who aced Tucker probably took it. Let's stop in at Bay's house and give him the word."

A gardener was spraying the rosebushes in front of Bay's house when we came up the driveway.

Dennis said, "Do you think he's using arsenic?"

I didn't answer. I had the feeling that his first choice for the man he wanted most to be put away was Turhan Bay. The kid was more on a mission than a hunt. He sat in the car; I went to the door.

When Bay opened it, he asked, "Trouble?"

I nodded. "Your cousin is dead."

"Dear God! What happened?"

I told him the whole story.

He said, "I can understand about the driver's license. He probably didn't have one. He had his license taken away from him several times in Chicago for drunk driving. But the money—?"

"Anyone who can kill can also steal," I said. "I

120

didn't tell the police about the money you gave him."

"Thank you for that," he said. He took a deep breath. "That crazy man. He always resented me for some strange reason. I could never understand why. I posted bail for him twice in Chicago. Thank you for stopping by."

In the car, as we drove off, Dennis said, "Do you remember what you told me at the beach, that Tucker would not be an asset to the mob?"

"I do."

"Maybe Gillete had the same thought. Getting rid of Tucker would make Gillete more acceptable. Firing him wouldn't be enough. Tucker could fink on him."

"That makes sense," I agreed.

"This case," he said, "is getting a little heavy for me. And my wife is getting nervous."

"Do you want out?"

"Not yet. But from now on, I'm carrying a gun. I've also got a nine millimeter Italian Galanti semi-automatic that holds twelve rounds if you want to borrow it."

"That's mighty heavy artillery, Dennis."

"For credit checks and divorce cases, yes. But not for *this.*"

"You win," I said.

When he dropped me off at the hotel, I headed for the bar. It had been a long time between drinks. The bar was cool and dim and filled with well-dressed people. I needed the change.

Half an hour later, when I came to the desk for my key, the clerk told me Lars had phoned. He had asked that I phone him back if I came in before six.

I phoned him from the room.

"You and your young friend are in the clear," he told me. "One of the neighbors saw the man go into that house carrying a bottle. From the description she gave us, I think we have a fix on the man. He's out of Las Vegas. His sister owns the title to that house. She lives in Venice now."

"I'm glad we're in the clear," I told him. "And I want to thank you for telling Slade about that fuss in Tessie's Tavern."

"Don't be so fucking petulant! I thought it was funny."

"Okay, okay! Are you going to stake out the woman's house? The man might be hiding there."

"You know Venice is not in our jurisdiction, Brock."

Mike was, I thought, but didn't voice. I said, "Thank you for calling."

"You're welcome. I'll get this paperwork cleared up soon. I can understand why you're pissed off at me. I'll call you as soon as it's cleaned up."

Considering the things I had learned about Mike since I came here, why was I so annoyed about Lars's sex life? Mike had lied to me about Gorman, and Gorman had suffered because of the lie. And it was possible that Crystal had lied about Lars. Even if she hadn't, being propositioned couldn't have been a new experience for her.

Joe Nolan had told me he had sorted out his priorities. It could be time for me to do the same. I had come here to avenge the death of the golden boy and learned he had turned into dross. It might be time for me to adjust to the real world. I had worked in the real world when I opened my office years ago down here.

My father, too, had worked in the real world. And I remembered what he had told me in my adolescence—nobody should get away with murder.

The killers kill and walk and kill again. That should not be.

I recorded the events of the day. Terrible Tim Tucker had lost his last match, but not intentionally this time. The man the neighbor had seen going into the deserted house carrying a bottle was from Las Vegas. Had Gillete finally been welcomed into the Family? Peter Scarlatti would know if he had.

I didn't intend to ask him. If Gillete had been accepted as a member, he was now in the Family. I wasn't.

Clauss, Tucker, and Gillete: that connection we had. Tucker was now dead. One obstacle to mob membership had been removed. A man as erratic as Clauss could be another. He could learn that it's easier to hide from the police than from the mob.

Young Clauss had still not been warned about his father. I drove to his apartment house after dinner. There was no answer to my ring. I pressed another button and a woman answered.

I told her I was a friend of Emil's, that something important had come up and I needed to get in touch with him.

He was visiting friends in New York, she told me, and would be gone for at least three months. He had sublet his apartment for that length of time.

Maybe somebody else had warned young Emil.

It was too nice a night to sit around in a hotel. I drove to Venice to learn if the boys from the West

Side station were doing their duty, staking out the house of the killer's sister.

If they were, they were not in evidence. All the cars parked on the block were unoccupied, all of the houses were lighted except for one. That could be her house.

From there to Tessie's Tavern. There were three men at the bar, a man and woman sitting at one of the two tables in the place.

"Mister Macho!" Tessie said. "Where's your sparring partner?"

"Dead," I said. "Murdered."

She stared at me.

"Today," I added. "Did he come in here often?"

She shook her head. "That day you had the fight with him was the first time I had ever seen him. Do the police know who did it?"

"They think they do, a man from Las Vegas. His sister lives about a block from here."

"Julie Woggon?"

"I don't know her name."

"It must be Julie. Her brother is a school bus driver in Vegas."

Lars had said the man was "out of Vegas." I had assumed from that, he had meant a hoodlum. He could be. It wasn't likely that he would admit it to his sister.

"Beer?" Tessie asked.

I nodded. "I'll have a glass of your best."

She filled it from a tap and set it in front of me. It was Becks dark. She asked, "Are you from out of town?"

I nodded. "San Valdesto. Denny told me you're a bowler."

"Yup. You a friend of his?"

124

"For all the years I lived down here."

She sighed. "That little bastard keeps hounding me to run a book here, like he does. But he gets the cop trade. I don't."

She went down to serve another customer. I sipped my beer.

When she came back, she asked, "Are you a friend of Sergeant Hovde's, too?"

I smiled, "Off and on. He's not easy to get along with."

"Off is the word for him," she said, "as in off limits. He spends more time down here than he does in his own town. I suppose it's because there are more whores down here."

"That could be," I agreed.

She went away again to serve another customer and got into a heated discussion with him. I finished my beer and left.

In my room I turned on the set for the local newscast, hoping there might be some new information on the death of Tim Tucker. There was none. Two-thirds of the half hour were devoted to the juvenile gang wars going on in central Los Angeles. Three of the gang members had been killed. A four-year-old girl had been killed in a drive-by shooting. There had been a witness who had taken down the license number of the car and informed the police. The youth had been caught. He had told the police it was all a mistake. He had been aiming at the infant's brother.

I recorded what I had learned tonight but didn't search for a pattern. I went to bed. A siren wailed from the street below. A noisy party was going on in the suite next door to me. But it had been an exhausting day. I slept.

CHAPTER FOURTEEN

The *Times* in the morning had a couple of paragraphs on the murder of Tucker in one of its inside pages. It mentioned his former career as a wrestler but nothing about the man who was suspected of killing him. The West Side station had apparently decided to give out this minimum information so as not to alert the man from Vegas. The *Times* had a lot of readers in Vegas.

Tucker had told his cousin he had to get out of town. Bay felt sure he had lied about that. Somebody had seen to it that if he had planned to leave town, he hadn't.

I looked up Julie Woggon in the phone book. The listing was in the name of J. Woggon. J. Woggon could be either male or female. Even in smug, snug San Valdesto, many of the widows and single women are so listed. Rapists rarely attack men. Women and children are their victims.

When Dennis came, he told me, "I brought the Galanti for you."

"I doubt if we'll need it on this trip," I said. I gave him Julie Woggon's address.

It was the same house that had been dark last night, as I had suspected, a small stucco house with a red tile roof. A thin gray-haired woman, wearing faded jeans and a sweat shirt, was watering some hanging plants on the small slat-roofed patio.

"More questions?" she asked as we came up the walk.

"We're not the police," I told her.

"Thank God for that! They questioned me for two hours yesterday and then the reporters came. Is that what you are?"

I shook my head. "I'm an investigator for the American Civil Liberties Union. One of the reporters who talked with you believes you were a victim of police harassment."

"I certainly was and I told them that. I guess they think everybody who lives in Las Vegas is a criminal. My brother drives a bus there. He drove a school bus in Santa Monica for years when we lived there."

"What's his first name?"

"Robert. Robert Jules Woggon. Do you know if the police have talked with him?"

I shook my head. "They don't confide in me."

"Do you think I might have grounds for a harassment suit? Not that I need the money, but I would love to give them some bad publicity."

"I doubt if you have grounds now," I said. "But it's possible your brother might have if he is falsely accused. I think it would be best if you waited for that."

"Probably," she agreed. "Thank you for your concern."

In the car, Dennis said, "I loved that ACLU bit. When did you dream up that one?"

"It so happens," I said coolly, "that I have been a member of the organization for over twenty years. Let's go to the station. I want to talk with Lars."

"Are you two buddies again?"

"Move it!" I said.

128

He parked on the shaded side of the station and stayed in the car. I went in.

Lars hadn't lied; his desk was crammed with papers. I told him what Julie Woggon had told me.

He sighed. "I *know* Woggon was a bus driver here. He was also a compulsive gambler. It was the school board that fired him. But it was his creditors who drove him out of town."

"Any word on him from the West Side station?"

"Yes. He left Vegas three days ago. He wasn't running a bus there. We haven't learned what he was doing, but he was living very high on the hog."

"Do you have a picture of him?"

"No. But there's one in the Santa Monica paper this morning." He smiled. "Brock, if you run into him and he offers to buy you a drink, don't take it."

"You have a macabre sense of humor, Lars."

"Whatever that means. Good hunting, buddy."

"Anything new?" Dennis asked when I came to the car.

I told him what Lars had told me.

"There goes Julie Woggon's harassment case," he said. "Let's pick up one of those pictures from the paper. I'll have it Xeroxed at Arden and hand out copies to the rest of the boys. We can use a few brownie points with the SMPD."

We picked up a paper at the rack in front of the station and drove to Arden Investigative Services, Inc. I didn't go in with him. I was sure that he hadn't told his boss that he was working with me.

When he came out again he brought a couple of enlarged copies with him. The picture in the paper had been only one column wide. This was clearer and it clearly wasn't a picture of Clauss.

He said, "We know what most of them look like now, don't we?"

"Most of whom?"

"The people we have talked with and questioned and seen. All but one, unless you've seen him."

"Which one?"

"Gillete."

"I've talked with him, but I've never seen him."

"Don't you think we should?"

"I suppose we should. For identification. But he knows my voice. You'll have to handle it alone. And Tucker could have told him who I am. He knew I wasn't what I claimed to be that first time I drove up there."

"If I handle it alone," he said, "I'll know what he looks like, but you won't. It'll have to be a picture. I'll be right back." He left the car.

Five minutes later, when he came back, he was carrying a wide leather belt with a large silver buckle.

"What in the hell is that contraption?" I asked him.

"The buckle is a camera. I've used it before. The boss is a camera nut. He invented it."

"I see. And you'll be wearing it around your waist. That should give you a good picture of his belly."

"The lens is angled upward," he explained. "I don't like to repeat myself—but I have used it before."

"Okay. Let's go."

Up the road to the Valley again. An illuminated neon sign on the roof of a savings and loan building on Ventura Boulevard informed the passersby

130

that the temperature was now ninety-eight degrees, the humidity seventy-two percent.

Dennis parked in the shade of a high shrub when we arrived at Gillete's house. It also served to screen the car from the view of anyone in the house. He buckled on the belt and left.

I got out of the car and went down beyond the far end of the shrubbery, hoping to catch some breeze from below.

There was no breeze and the sun's rays were higher than the shrubbery. I went back to stand next to the car.

He was smiling when he came down the road five minutes later.

"You lucked out," I guessed.

He nodded. "I told him Tucker was a friend of mine and that his funeral would be tomorrow. I suggested that he say a few words at the mortuary. He told me he was busy tomorrow."

"Good work. That completes the cast, doesn't it?"

He shook his head. "I forgot one—that lawyer, Winthrop Loeb. All we have is his license number."

"Loeb next," I said. "Let's go."

We stopped for gas in the Valley. While he filled the tank, I looked up Loeb's office in the station phone book. It was in Beverly Hills.

"Have you dreamed up a story to tell Loeb?" I asked.

"Some of it. I think better on my feet."

Tiger, tiger, burning bright . . . He was making me feel like an anachronism.

The office was in a recently remodeled five-story

building on Sunset. When he parked on the lot I suggested that I go in with him.

He shook his head. "I plan to use a phony name."

"I've got a lot of those," I said.

"And a famous name. I'll bet that half of the men and all of the sports fans in this county remember you from when you were with the Rams. Loeb could be one of them."

"That's nonsense," I said.

"Trust me," he said. "Even my mother-in-law remembers you."

"You win," I said.

He went to the office. I went shopping. I was running out of clean shorts and socks.

I was back in the car a few minutes before he returned. He was smiling again. Loeb's secretary, he told me, had been very uncooperative at first, but when he mentioned that it was Gillete who had suggested that he come to get advice from her boss, she had relented.

"Advice?"

"Right! I fed him a story about these rich friends of mine from San Francisco who want to invest in redevelopment property down here. We have an appointment for tomorrow morning at nine o'clock."

"Dennis," I said, "Loeb probably phoned Gillete right after you left the office. I hope to hell you don't plan to show up for the appointment."

"Of course not! But it should throw both of them off balance, shouldn't it? You know—keep 'em discombobulated."

"Smart move," I said. That had always been one of my ploys. Maybe I wasn't an anachronism.

Arden had their own photo-processing equipment. It was close to noon when we got there. We waited on the lot until we saw his boss leave for lunch.

"He'd probably charge me for the photos," he explained. "He wanted to charge me for borrowing the camera. But his wife was in the office and she shamed him out of that."

He handed me the pictures when he returned to the car. "The one who looks human is Loeb," he said. "The other is Gillete."

Loeb's face was aquiline, adorned with a trim Vandyke beard and piercing dark eyes. He would have been successful, I was sure, at selling junk bonds to gullible widows. Gillete could have been a club fighter. He was swarthy, partially bald, scowling, with a shadow of a beard no razor could erase, à la Richard Nixon.

It seemed clear to me he was not what the family would welcome in their current period of enlightenment. That was a comforting thought.

"Where now?" Dennis asked.

"Let's go to the station to find out if Lars has anything new to tell us. We can stop at the sandwich shop on the way."

Lars was at the shop, alone in a booth. We sat down across from him. "Anything new on Woggon?" I asked.

He shook his head. "And what have you two been doing?"

I told him where we had been and what we had done since we left the station.

"Jesus!" he said. "The way you guys operate."

"We don't have jurisdiction problems," I explained.

133

He scowled. "Was that a shot?"

"No. It was an explanation. Neither of the men we talked with today are in your jurisdiction. Tucker was. And who found him for you?"

"Okay, okay!" He finished his sandwich and drank the rest of his coffee and stood up. "As soon as I learn anything, you'll be the first to know."

"Thanks, Lars," I said.

He nodded and went out, still scowling.

"We're starting to get the connections between all of the suspects, aren't we?" Dennis asked while we ate our own lunch.

"So far."

"It's costing you a lot of money."

"Yes. But I'm not quitting."

"Because Gregory was your friend?"

"That's why I came here. It's not why I'm staying."

It *was* costing me money. Mike's mortuary bill and all the expenses I had incurred since then added up to more money than I had earned in six months when I was working my trade in Beverly Hills.

And it was probably a lack of money that had got Mike killed, either through a blackmail attempt or trying to lure new customers to support his own talent. Drugs were no big business in this country, as liquor had been in the long-gone prohibition days. In both periods, the pros resented competition. The man who had killed my father had been a dealer. Urban kids were dropping out of school to act as couriers for this scum. The kids usually wound up in jail, the dealers too rarely. They could afford expensive lawyers. The kids couldn't.

"What are you thinking about?" Dennis asked.

"About what one of Bay's followers told me about his philosophy. She told me he believed this planet of ours can't be the only planet in the universe. There have to be some planets where the citizens have advanced beyond lust for money and constant wars. Does that make sense to you?"

"I've been thinking along the same line," he said. "At least about the money. My dad went through the Depression. That was supposed to be a bad time. But he looks back on it with fondness now."

I stood up. "Let's go back and talk with Julie Woggon. Maybe she's heard from her brother."

She was still out on her patio, varnishing two redwood benches and a redwood picnic table.

She smiled at me. "If you've come to talk with my brother, he should be here soon. He's at the Santa Monica police station now. But one of your people phoned a few minutes ago to tell me he would soon be released."

"My people?"

She nodded. "From the ACLU. He thinks we might have a harassment case. You know, putting Robert's picture in the paper and bothering me."

"What happened?"

"He was visiting my father in Eureka. My father is a deputy sheriff up there. And he was there when that Tucker person was killed."

"That's great news," I said.

"Do you still want to talk with Robert?"

I shook my head. "There's no need to now."

"Well, I do want to thank you for all the help

you've given me. I phoned the ACLU right after you left this morning."

"Good luck on the harassment case," I said. And thought: *I'll hold my thumbs.*

CHAPTER FIFTEEN

Dennis was smiling as we walked to the car. "Cowboy Hovde now has egg all over his ugly face. I wish I had been there to see it."

I held my tongue.

"Another dead end," he said.

"Dennis," I explained to him patiently, "most of the murder cases I worked on were *loaded* with dead ends. They are not credit checks or divorces or guard duty, like Arden handles. They are dead ends and blind alleys."

He said nothing.

"Don't sulk," I said. "That will be your lecture for today."

"I think I'll go home," he said wearily. "I've cost you too much and delivered too little."

"That's not true. You've been a big help. Back to credit checks now?"

He shook his head. "I still have a few days of vacation left. If you need me, holler."

It was a quiet trip to the hotel. When I reached into the backseat for my purchases, he said, "Take the gun, too. Consider it a present from my wife. She insisted that I get rid of it. One of my macho uncles gave it to me when I started to work at Arden."

"Thanks," I said.

I also had gone the Arden route for eating money during my days down here. Murder investigations paid for by wealthy clients paid a lot better, despite the fact that they brought me into trouble with the police. Neither had paid enough for me to marry Jan. I had to wait for my uncle to die before I could afford her.

It had been different when I moved to San Valdesto; they could use free help. That was my edge there.

The desk clerk told me a man had phoned around noon and asked that I call him back. He hadn't given his name, only his phone number.

I knew the number; it was Peter Scarlatti's. I phoned him from the room.

He had, he told me, done some research on Gillete after my visit and my phone call. "He's got a man named Clauss working for him now. Watch out for him! He's a real psycho."

"I know that. But I didn't know you cared."

"Don't be cute. If it hadn't been for Puma, I'd have died in my youth. And I remember what you did for his wife and kid."

"Be sure you don't tell the Feds that. Is there anything else you can tell me about Clauss?"

"Not yet. But we're looking into it. One thing this country doesn't need is disorganized crime. Tell me, Brock, just between us, are you the man who sent Tucker into the great beyond?"

"Poison? Me?"

"A dumb question," he admitted. "Be careful now and carry a big stick."

"I will. I just inherited a Galanti."

"That's a big stick," he said. "Good luck."

I had done something for Joe Puma. I had convinced his wife and son that he had not been guilty of blackmail, though he had. And been killed because he had. Peter had sent them a Christmas check every year when he became an adult.

Dead ends and blind alleys, but the search was narrowing. Luplow was dead; that had been a blind alley not connected with this case. Gorman had been cleared and Carlos Minatti had been in Fresno. So far as I knew, he was no longer a suspect. Tucker was dead. All we had left was Clauss, a maverick, a drug dealer and killer.

It didn't seem likely to me that if Clauss had conned Mike into meeting him on the beach late at night, Mike would not have had enough sense to stay away or suggest a change to a more populated area. Unless Mike was in dire need of a jolt.

I stretched out on the bed after dinner to take a nap. I was deep in a dream too salacious to record when the phone wakened me. It was Lars.

"That Woggon, the bus driver, has been cleared," he told me. "And now his attorney is threatening to hit us with a harassment suit."

I didn't mention my part in that. I said, "Well, you know how lawyers are, always after the fast buck."

"Right! This week's been a real downer. Did you learn anything on Clauss?"

"A little."

"I've cleaned up my paperwork, so I'm available for part-time duty again."

"Why don't you come here?" I suggested. "We can have a drink and talk about our next move."

"I thought you'd never ask," he said.

He was dressed in his Sunday best when I met him in the lobby, but he still looked like a mean, tough cop.

Over our drinks I told him what Shorty had told

me about Clauss's gun collection, including the two shotguns, and his belief that Clauss would not desert his Santa Monica home turf. I added what Peter Scarlatti had confirmed; that Clauss was working for Gillete, something we had suspected. I told him about the Gillete connection with attorney Winthrop Loeb.

"You and the wimp have sure been busy," he said.

"Lars, Dennis is not a wimp. He was a big help to me."

"Was?"

"Was. He told me he hadn't been earning his pay. I have the feeling that he's not ready for the heavy stuff. His wife insisted he get rid of his fifteen-shot Galanti. He gave it to me."

"A Galanti? Do you have a permit for that?"

"I have a gun permit, but not for that one."

"Maybe I can finagle you one. A gun like that could put a lot of holes into Clauss. Let's have another drink."

We had that and a few more. I was woozy when he left. I phoned room service and ordered a pot of coffee.

We had all the connections, Bay with Nolan and Tucker, Loeb, Gillete and Tucker and Clauss. The connection with Turhan Bay was doubtful.

Lars hated crooked cops. That might be the wrong reason to concentrate on Clauss. But my conviction was growing that he had to be our number-one choice for the murder of Mike Gregory.

My addled brain rebelled. I went to bed and tried to sleep. Nausea stirred in me. I walked slowly and carefully to the toilet and vomited. That helped; I finally fell asleep.

The business section in the *Times* reported that two more financial firms were being investigated by the Feds, a brokerage in Newport Beach, a savings and loan firm in Beverly Hills. The millionaire electronic preachers were being investigated by the IRS. That was long overdue.

My stomach was back to normal. I ate a full breakfast. Lars would not be available until this afternoon. I decided to make a call on my friend at E.F. Hutton.

He smiled as I entered his cubicle. "I hope you're going to tell me you've decided to switch your account."

"I've been considering it. You have an office in San Valdesto."

He nodded. "Tell 'em I sent you. Brock, you have never been a financial wizard. And discount brokers don't give their customers investment advice."

"I've learned that to my regret," I lied. "But that isn't the only reason I came. Do you know an attorney named Winthrop Loeb?"

He nodded. "But not well. I've been to a couple of parties where I talked with him briefly and listened to a speech of his at a financial seminar. There is a rumor going around that he might be tied up with the local Mafia."

"Not quite yet. At the moment he seems to be tied up with a hoodlum named Arnold Gillete."

"Never heard of him." He frowned. "Is all this connected with Mike Gregory's murder?"

"It could be. So far it's just a hunch I've been working on. The word I got, the SEC is investigating Loeb."

"That I didn't hear. What do you want from me?"

"I thought maybe a financial wizard like you could get me some information on the Gillete-Loeb connection."

"Brock, I am not a detective. And I sure as hell don't want to get on this Gillete's hit list. Be reasonable!"

"You could be discreet about it," I explained. "You wouldn't have to get involved with him directly. You could ask around among your peers. They might know about the connection."

"That I could do," he admitted. "And if I learn anything I'm sure you will consider switching your account to our office in San Valdesto."

"Of course I will."

Brokers . . . I had saved him all that alimony money and now he wanted me to do *him* a favor. Brokers . . .

Lars had given me the name last night of a cantankerous old man who had been a close friend of Clauss until Clauss had been fired. That had ended their relationship and also the man's regard for police officers. But he *might* talk with me, Lars had suggested.

He spent most of his days on the small park above the bluff that fronted on the ocean in Santa Monica. I drove there.

The benches in the park were mostly occupied by couples. At the far end, a thin old man attired in denim pants, a red field jacket, and a blue baseball cap, was sitting alone and staring down at the beach.

I parked across the street and walked over to the bench.

"Mr. Grosskopf?" I asked.

He looked up at me suspiciously and nodded. "Do I know you?"

"No. I'm trying to find a man named Emil Clauss. I was told that you knew him."

"Are you a cop?"

I shook my head. "I'm a friend of his son. But he's out of town right now."

"If you're a friend of his," he said, "you can't be a friend of his father's. Or are you?"

"Quite the opposite. I think he killed a friend of mine. But the Santa Monica police don't seem to be working very hard on the case. I guess they've lost interest in it."

"Was your friend that man who was found on the beach with his face blasted off?"

I nodded.

"That could be chalked up to Clauss," he said. "The man's turned into a mental case. Sit down."

I sat next to him and he told me the story of their history. Both he and Clauss had been members of the National Rifle Association. They had often gone hunting together. Clauss was a young and single man then. But after he was married, his disposition soured. Like many former philanderers, he was intensely jealous.

"His wife's a saint," he said. "I tried to reason with him. But he is one stubborn bastard. He always had a macho complex. Most hunters do. That's why I quit the NRA."

"Do you have any idea of where he might be now?"

"None. But I could ask around. I'm getting tired of sitting up here staring at those young girls down on the beach. I'm sure they wouldn't be interested in a horny old man."

"Some older women might."

He sighed. "I've been thinking along those lines. I've decided to join one of those senior citizen clubs. What's your name?"

"Brock Callahan. I'm staying at the Beverly Hills Hotel."

He stared at me. "Didn't you used to play with the Dodgers?"

"Nope. The Rams."

"I never followed them," he said. "If I learn anything that might help you find that weirdo, I'll give you a call."

"Do that. If I'm not there, phone the Santa Monica station."

"That would be my last resort," he said.

CHAPTER SIXTEEN

It was still well short of the time I was due to pick up Lars. My chances of spotting Emil Clauss walking the streets of his hometown in daylight were slim. He knew that he was being hunted. For all I knew, he could take Tucker's place as a guest at the Valley residence of Arnold Gillete.

But I made the grand tour from Santa Monica to Venice along the least inhabited streets and came back to the station fifteen minutes early.

There, the desk sergeant told me that Lars had phoned twice this morning but I had been out. He had been recruited with other officers for a stakeout on a house suspected of harboring a criminal.

"Emil Clauss?"

He shook his head. "Some Chicano drug dealer."

Back to my novice days, when I had worked alone in my own way, without the aid of a belt-buckle camera. There were some contradictory lies to be clarified. I drove to Brentwood, to the home of Turhan Bay. He was out in front, waxing his Jaguar.

"More trouble?" he asked.

"Nothing violent," I told him. "I have a feeling that a man named Joe Nolan has lied to me about you. Do you know him?"

He nodded. "I suppose he could be called my broker. I bought three hundred shares of a mutual fund from one of his junior partners several months ago. I've let the dividends roll over and now have three hundred and twelve shares."

"How much are they worth now?"

"A little over three thousand dollars."

"Does your wife have an account there, too?"

He shook his head. "She has been with E.F. Hutton for years. What's this all about?"

"Nolan told me that your account there was around a million dollars."

"The man's insane! Why would he tell you that?"

"That's what I hope to find out. I think he was trying to lead me down a blind alley."

"Does it have anything to do with what happened to Tim?"

"I doubt it. But it could have something to do with Mike's murder."

"Murder? Nolan?"

"I'm sure he didn't kill Mike. But there's a strong possibility that he might know who did."

"Have the police learned anything about who killed Tim?"

"Not yet. They probably suspect, as I do, that the man I told you about, Emil Clauss, killed Mike and your cousin."

He nodded. "I phoned my detective friend at the West Side station. He had the same opinion. But he explained to me that that was a Santa Monica investigation."

"It is. I'm working with them now."

"Good luck," he said. "I liked Mike as much as Crystal told me you do."

From there to Beverly Hills. Nolan was in his

glass-enclosed office when I entered, talking with a secretary. When she left, I went in.

"And what brings *you* here?" he asked.

Seconds passed, while he studied me. And then he smiled. "Brock, Bay has a very modest account here. But, as you probably don't know, his wife has a very big account at Hutton. And she is a woman who doesn't have long to live. I have good reason to believe that when she dies and Bay inherits, he will transfer that account to me."

"Why would he?"

He smiled. "Because I just happen to know something about him that his followers don't."

"That he's gay?"

The smile faded; he stared at me. "Where did you learn that?"

"From one of my sources. I'm sure the SEC would be interested to learn that you are contemplating blackmail."

"It would be your word against mine, Brock."

"Mine and Bay's," I pointed out. "Who do you think the Feds would believe? The next move is yours, Joe. Give it a lot of thought."

He was still staring at me before I turned and walked out. It was possible that he would call my bluff. But he never had in those nights we had played poker together.

He had changed his story from the million-dollar Bay account to a future million-dollar Bay account. It was likely that both stories were false. The story he had confirmed about Bay's sexual preference was true.

But where had he learned it? The logical choice seemed to be Tim Tucker. It was possible that he had gotten more than the two thousand dollars he had picked up from his cousin. Tucker could have gained at least that much if he had told Nolan.

I drove back to Brentwood. Bay was still out on the driveway, now checking the tire pressure on his newly polished car. I couldn't think of any tactful way to open the subject. Tact had never been one of my virtues. I gave him the verbatim account of my dialogue with Joe Nolan.

"Damn him!" he said. "Where did he learn that?"

"Maybe from your cousin. Did he blackmail you, too?"

He sighed. "He did. But I have never even spoken with Joe Nolan. The only person I have ever talked with there was one of the junior partners and that was on the phone."

"There's a strong chance that you will never have to talk to Nolan after he digests what I told him. He could be in deep trouble."

"Thank you for that. I have a number of my flock who are gay. But, unfortunately, most of them aren't."

"One thing we're sure of . . ." I said. "Your cousin can no longer slander you. And I have the firm feeling that Nolan is now playing in company too rough for him. I plan to make that clear to him. He's the weak link in the chain."

"Good luck," he said. "As for what he told you about my wife, he'd have a long wait for his money. She's in a lot better health than I am."

I drove to the Santa Monica station from there and Lars was at his desk.

"How did the stakeout go?" I asked him.

"Successfully. What's by you new?"

I didn't tell him about the sexual angle on my

visits to Bay and Nolan, only that I had talked with them and learned that Nolan had lied about Bay's million-dollar account. And then I told him about my park-bench dialogue with Grosskopf.

"Nolan could be the key," he said. "But we would need stronger evidence on his financial shenanigans."

"I can work that end. I told Grosskopf to call here if he can't get in touch with me."

"I hope that old sourpuss doesn't get too nosy. Clauss might hear about it and I'm sure he hates Grosskopf. Clauss must know almost every hoodlum and stoolie in this town. Do you plan to go cruising this afternoon?"

"Nope. I had enough of that this morning. Speaking of stoolies, are you ready for a weird thought that I've just dreamed up?"

"I'll listen."

"If we can't find Clauss, maybe we can get him to come looking for me. You know, spread the word here and there—?"

"Brock, he must know by now that we are both looking for him."

"Right. Gillete probably does, too. And one thing he sure as hell doesn't want is Clauss in the can, where he can make a deal with the DA."

"That's too tricky for me," Lars said, "and doubtful police procedure."

"It's tricky," I agreed.

He frowned. "What is it with you, a death wish? Clauss isn't likely to miss a target as big as you."

"Or you."

"You think he's kooky enough to kill a cop?"

I smiled. "There's a way to find out."

"You are a strange one," he said. "But I'll have

to admit you're right. I've been shot at a few times."

"Did you go to their funerals?"

"You bastard! I never killed anyone who didn't deserve it."

"Clauss deserves it. You put in what time you can here in town. I'm going back to Beverly Hills."

I stopped in at Heinie's for lunch, and used his office phone to call Gillete. I tried to pitch my voice higher this time than when he had phoned me.

When he answered, I said, "This is just a friendly warning, Mr. Gillete. There's a private eye in town who is determined to railroad Emil Clauss into the can. I think you should warn him."

"Why should I? And who the hell are you?"

"A friend of Emil's and possibly an associate later."

A fairly long silence. Then, "What's the private eye's name?"

"I don't know it. Clauss might. The peeper is working with a Santa Monica cop. That's all I know now. If you're not interested in Clauss, forget what I said."

"I already have," he said, and hung up.

Was it the word "associate," I wondered, that had prompted his momentary silence? Would he assume that since he had dumped Tucker, he might be invited into the big time?

That Lars and his proper police procedure . . . How often had he been guided by that? Though he would never admit it, he was a cowboy cop. He had seen too many killers walk and too many criminals get minimum sentences. He had saved the taxpayers a lot of money on cases that would have clogged the courts for years if the guilty could afford expensive attorneys.

The only phone calls I had received, the desk clerk told me, were this morning's calls from Lars. There was no need to record what I had learned today; the connection was complete.

All of them were fervent followers of the American dream, *money*. Whether it was blackmail or the swindle Bay had run in Chicago or the Mafia or cops on the take, it was money. The love of money is the root of all evil.

I was stretched on the bed, trying to nap, when the phone rang.

"Mr. Callahan?" a woman asked.

"Yes."

"I'm calling from Meridian Hospital in Santa Monica. A patient here has asked me to phone you. He wants you to come here. His name is Rudolph Grosskopf."

"What happened to him?"

"He has a broken arm and some bruises. He told the doctor he was walking down an alley and stumbled over something. We have the feeling that might not be true."

"Tell him I'm on the way," I said.

He had stumbled in an alley? Why would he ask for me? He must have been doing what he had promised to do when he and I talked on the bench —asking around. It was likely that he had asked the wrong person.

CHAPTER SEVENTEEN

I didn't phone Lars. Grosskopf, I was sure, would not be as cooperative with Lars as he would with me. Cops were not his favorite people.

He was in a two-bed room, but there was no other occupant. He had dark bruises below both eyes. He grinned as I entered.

"Don't tell me it could have been worse," he said. "That's what the doctor told me. It wasn't the guy who hit me that broke my arm. I broke it when I fell. He hit me twice and I went down. Then some woman started screaming at him from the end of the alley."

"What were you doing in the alley?"

"Taking a leak. Old guys have to pee a lot. I had a couple of beers in this bar and was walking toward home when one of the guys from the bar followed me down the alley."

"Do you know who he is?"

"Not by name. I've seen him there before. He's a little guy, but he sure has a wallop. He was wearing blue corduroy pants and a blue work shirt. He had an earring in his left ear."

"Were you asking about Clauss in the bar?"

He nodded. "With the bartender. This guy must have overheard it. Would you tell the nurse I want to leave now? I don't like hospitals."

"I'll go and ask her. What's the name of that bar?"

"The Dungeon."

I phoned the station and Lars was there. I told him where I was and what had happened.

"I'll meet you at The Dungeon," he said. "You tell Grosskopf to stay where he is. We might need him for identification."

When I came back to his room, he asked, "What did the nurse say?"

"I didn't ask her. You'll have to stay here for a while. You might be needed for identification. I'm going to that bar."

"Damn it!" he said. "If that little bastard is there and you bring him here, maybe you could hold him so I could give him a couple of shots."

I smiled at him. "Take it easy, Rudolph. Stay cool, man!"

Lars was pulling up in his car when I arrived at The Dungeon. We went in together.

There were two men standing at the bar, two others sitting at a table at the far end. One of them fit the description Rudolph had given me. He smiled as we got closer.

He said, "Look who is here. Cowboy Hovde!"

"Don't get lippy with me, Ernie. I eat men your size."

"Not this one. You don't have to Miranda me. I don't like finks and I don't like cops who are trying to railroad Emil."

"You are admitting you beat up an old man?"

"I gave that fink a couple of shots. He was exposing himself in a public place."

"But you didn't report it."

"To the cops. I would have reported it to Emil. *He* was a good cop."

"Do you know where he is now?"

154

He shook his head. "And even if I did, I sure as hell wouldn't squeal on him."

Lars sighed. "Okay. Let's go."

"Go where?"

"To the station. You've admitted you assaulted an old man. While we're at the station, I can check your record."

"Aw, come on, Lars!"

"Ernie, your friend Clauss was never a good cop. And right now he is the major suspect in two murders."

Ernie stared at him. "Murder? Emil?"

"Yes. And that old man you slugged was once his best friend. Maybe you don't know that Clauss was fired because he killed an unarmed drug dealer."

"I didn't," Ernie admitted.

"It's all true," Lars said. "I'll ask you once more. Do you know where Clauss is now?"

Ernie shook his head. "I swear to you I don't. And if he's that heavy now, I ain't about to ask."

"That's up to you. The old guy was asking, but he has guts. And he knows that Clauss has to be put away."

Ernie looked doubtfully at the man with him.

The man said, "I'm not a Clauss fan. What the sergeant told you is true. Emil's turned into a weirdo, the word I got." He looked at Lars. "We'll do what we can, but don't expect any miracles. This is the wrong end of town for asking questions."

Lars was smiling when we went out. "Feisty little bastard, isn't he? He was a pretty fair bantam-weight boxer a few years ago. I'm going home from here. I doubt if Grosskopf wants to talk with me. Did you learn anything this afternoon?"

I shook my head. I told him about my phone call to Gillete.

"Maybe that will bring Clauss out. Keep your gun handy."

Rudolph was getting dressed when I came into his room. The doctor, he told me, had given him permission to go home. A second X ray had revealed that the bone in his lower arm had not been broken, only cracked.

"Next time you leave the house, be more careful," I warned him. "You could be a target for Clauss. And you're not armed."

"I will be next time," he said. "I could always outshoot Emil, rifle or pistol. That man's left-handed and about as accurate as an armless midget."

"Clauss's best weapon is a shotgun, a sawed-off shotgun. It's hard to miss with one of those. Matter of fact, he has two shotguns."

"He needs 'em. What happened at The Dungeon?"

I gave him the gist of it. I asked him if he had brought enough money to pay his way out.

He nodded. "Medicare will pay most of it. I can handle the rest." He shook his head. "You know, when this country was sane, I could get a room at the Ritz in New York for about a fourth of what this room will cost. It's not my America anymore."

I drove him home. The place had obviously been built many years ago, a cement-block building, fronted by a concrete parking space, with a tile roof and narrow windows, protected by wrought-iron bars.

"I call it my fortress," he said. "We need 'em down here."

156

Back at the hotel, I propped a chair under the knob of the door before I took my shower. Clauss obviously frightened me more than he did Grosskopf.

The attack on Grosskopf by Ernie couldn't have been dictated by Gillete. He had probably never heard of the man, and it had been too soon after my phone call for that. But there had been time enough for Gillete to warn Clauss.

Nolan hadn't called. Perhaps he was dreaming up new fantasies for me. He would have made a lousy private eye; he didn't know when to lie or how to do it.

Frustration had made me foolhardy. Phoning Gillete had been a dumb and dangerous move. The hunter had now become the hunted. What would have been a threat to a rational man would be only a challenge to Clauss.

It was probable, when I went down to dinner, that I was the only guest in the long and distinguished history of the Beverly Hills Hotel who had ever carried a fifteen-shot Galanti in a shoulder holster into their dining room.

No booze tonight. I planned to go hunting in the forlorn hope that Clauss was a night crawler and still in town. I comforted myself with the knowledge that a moving target is the most difficult target to hit.

Down the mean streets of the town Raymond Chandler had labeled Bay City, concentrating on the saloons. From there to Venice and back to Santa Monica.

I was luckier on my second trip past The Dungeon. Through the wide front window I could see the blue shirt of the man I knew only as Ernie.

I parked in front and went in. There were three customers in the place, all standing at the bar, all male. Ernie turned toward the doorway as I came in.

"More trouble?" he asked.

"Not for you. I'm not a cop. My name is Brock Callahan."

He nodded. "I thought I recognized you this afternoon. You must have put on weight since you were with the Rams."

"A little, I guess."

"That Hovde!" he said. "He brings out the worst in me."

"Me, too, quite often. But everything he told you was true. His son told me that Clauss beat up his wife so badly she was taken to a hospital and was put into intensive care. His son won't have anything to do with him."

"Jesus! What's his beef with you?"

"I think he killed a friend of mine. And it's possible I'm next on his list."

He took a sip of his beer. "I asked around a little today. All I learned so far from a fink who's been wrong before is that Clauss is steamed about some private eye who's out to nail him."

"You're standing next to him, Ernie. That's what I was, after I left the Rams."

"Then what in the hell are you doing down here? This is Clauss country, man."

"That's what I'm doing down here, looking for him. Only this time I'm armed. Thanks for what you told me."

"You're welcome," he said. "Don't lead with your chin."

It had not been a fruitless trip. I now knew that

Clauss had been alerted by Gillete. There was the possibility that Gillete had ordered him to cool it. He had to realize that Clauss's erratic behavior was dangerous folly. Mavericks are not the kind of soldiers that well-run hoodlum organizations recruit. Nor do they tolerate personal vendettas.

But Clauss, in his present state of mind, was not likely to take rational advice. That was all right with me. I didn't have the ammo to take on an army. One on one against Clauss would be my preference.

I drove past the fortress of Rudolph Grosskopf before heading for the hotel. The narrow windows showed no light from within. All seemed serene under a full moon. Maybe the old curmudgeon would find a female partner mature and tolerant enough to appreciate him. I hoped so. He was my kind of man.

I had given my address to too many people. Even Clauss could know it by now. I phoned the Crest Motel in Santa Monica and got a reservation. I phoned Mrs. Casey and told her where I would be and asked her to notify Jan if she called.

I put a chair under the knob of my door again, and laid my Galanti on the bedside table.

Tomorrow I would set up camp in Clauss country.

CHAPTER EIGHTEEN

"Heading for home?" the clerk asked in the morning. "That's a beautiful town you live in, Mr. Callahan."

"It is," I agreed. "Unfortunately, I have to go to Cleveland first and spend several weeks there."

I unloaded my luggage in my room at the Crest Motel before phoning Lars to give him the address.

He said, "I phoned you this morning and the clerk told me you were on your way to Cleveland."

"I lied to him. I didn't want Clauss to come busting in there. Anything new?"

"Nothing worth repeating. I'm still buried in paperwork."

"Well, you now know where I am if you need me."

After breakfast, I phoned my broker friend at Hutton. I told him my new address and asked if he had learned anything about Winthrop Loeb.

He said, "You've already told me more about him than I knew. I'm working on something else, what you might call a line of inquiry."

"What is it?"

"Nothing I care to discuss right now. If I confirm what I suspect, I'll pass it on. It requires some finesse and might defame an innocent man. By the way, I called San Valdesto this morning and gave them your name as a prospective client."

"I forgive you."

"Brock, one favor deserves another."

The alimony I had saved him! One favor deserves another? Brokers are strange people . . .

I looked up Rudolph Grosskopf in the phone book and called him. I identified myself and asked him, "How are you feeling today?"

"Better. I sure as hell blew it yesterday, didn't I?"

"You paid for it. And you definitely helped us yesterday by identifying the man who assaulted you. I talked with him at The Dungeon last night and he gave me some information that might help."

"What's that little bastard's name?"

"Mr. Grosskopf, it wouldn't be a smart move for you to get involved with him. He's a former boxer. I also don't think you should involve yourself in a murder case. You could get hurt asking questions about Clauss in your neighborhood."

He sighed. "I suppose you're right. I learned that the hard way yesterday. Well, I've got some lines out to some people who might know where Clauss is now. They can report to me here. I guess that would be safer, huh?"

"It would." I told him my new address and phone number and suggested he report to me if he learned anything from his sources.

"I will," he said. "I trust you. But not cops."

"All cops aren't like Clauss, Mr. Grosskopf."

"I know," he said wearily. "I suppose I've turned sour since he went bananas. I don't have any close friends anymore."

"Maybe you need a female friend. They're more dependable. This area is loaded with widows."

"I've noticed that, reading the obituary page. As

soon as Emil is put away and I can get out and around again, I'll try to find me one. Good luck on your hunt."

I hadn't done any walking or exercising since I came down here, except for the walk on the beach with Crystal. I had told all the people I trusted where I was staying.

I put on my walking shoes and went out into a sunny day moderated by a cooling breeze from the ocean. Last night I had traveled the mean streets. But not today. Clauss could have bought a toupee to cover his baldness and dyed his white eyebrows. The likelihood of his mingling with the solid citizens was remote. But he was a kinky man and I had no other leads to pursue.

Grocers first; the man had to eat. Motel lobbies and sporting goods stores, two pool halls and a bowling alley. No Clauss. The last stop was only a few blocks from Crystal's house. I walked there and rang her doorbell. There was no answer.

From there to the beach, to the place where Mike's body had been found. What had that poor bastard been doing there at two o'clock in the morning?

I thought of what Nolan had told me that day he came to my room. He had tried to steer me on to Turhan Bay as a suspect. Mike, he had suggested might have learned about Bay's relationship with Crystal. He had labeled her a former hooker. Wouldn't that, he had suggested, lose Bay his followers?

His lies had been so transparent they had to be the impulse of the moment. In his talk with Chief Denzler at the Santa Monica Department, he had learned that Mike's murder would get a minimum of investigation. That could have been comforting to him, but he knew, when he saw me at the mortuary, that I would take a more emotional interest in Mike's death.

He had explained that lack of Department interest to me, which was the truth. The lie that followed, on the mortuary parking lot, about his hope that I would investigate the murder was false. It had taken him the rest of the afternoon to concoct that story about the wealth of Turhan Bay and the lie that Bay was one of his major accounts.

That farce in his office about knowing something about Bay that he could use to get his wife's account could have been another impulse of the moment, another lie. I, with my big mouth, might have told him what he *hadn't* known about Bay.

I walked back to the motel for my car. I had lunch at Heinie's and walked from there the two blocks to Nolan's office. He was alone in his cubicle today. I went in.

He looked up and smiled at me. "You win, Brock. Blackmail is not my game. I was just about to phone you and tell you that. Were you really going to report me to the SEC?"

"Not unless I had to. Tell me, when did you learn about Bay's sexual preference?"

He smiled again. "When you told me." He took a deep breath. "The sad fact is that one of my young partners has got himself involved in some financial shenanigans the SEC might decide to be illegal. Neither I nor my attorney believe they have a case. But if you brought the SEC into it, this young man's promising career could go down the drain."

164

Bullshit, I thought. I said, "That would be unfortunate."

"Very unfortunate. Do you know if the Santa Monica police have any information on Mike's case?"

I shook my head. "I guess I'll have to go it alone. You were right about their lack of interest."

Another phony smile. "I don't *always* lie, Brock."

"I can guess why. You're not very good at it."

"I haven't had much practice at it," he lied.

Back at the motel, the kids were splashing in the pool, adults were stretched out on deck chairs. When would I return to that? Not yet, I knew. Emil Clauss had become an obsession.

The clerk told me I'd had no calls. Lars was probably still swamped in his paperwork. As I had told Nolan, I would probably have to go it alone.

I thought back to my dialogue with him. His story about the problems his junior partner was having might have seemed credible to some. But not to anyone who had heard him lie as often as I had.

He had asked if the Santa Monica police had any suspect on Mike's murder. To the innocent that would be a routine question about a friend. My feeling was that his concern was whether the Department had learned anything that would connect him with the killer, however loosely.

He could be the final connection in this chain, from Loeb to Gillete to Claus—and now Nolan. Gillete and Winthrop Loeb were definitely connected. Was Loeb the attorney Nolan had said was his when I talked with him today. Peter Scarlatti had told me that Loeb had deserted his criminal practice and gone into financial manipulations and was currently being investigated by the SEC.

It was possible that the SEC's case was as weak as Nolan and his attorney had claimed. My revealing Nolan's blackmail threat might add enough substance to make the SEC case stronger.

But I had no proof that Nolan had mentioned blackmail to me. Any defense attorney would make that clear to a judge or jury. I knew and Nolan knew that he had suggested blackmail. That was a fact we both knew, but he certainly would not admit. His word would be as good as mine in court.

Too much time had been spent in the frustrating and fruitless hunt for Clauss. It was time to concentrate on the Nolan connection. At least I knew where he was and I doubted that he was armed.

The major chicaneries of the time were being revealed almost every day in the newspapers and the tube. Several of them had included murder and this could add to the list.

Connecting financial shenanigans to the death of Mike Gregory would not be an easy chore for me. As my Hutton friend had told me, I was not a financial wizard.

It wasn't easy for me to believe that Mike had been guilty of blackmail. But that was the way this case was shaping up.

CHAPTER NINETEEN

Kids played in the pool outside, their parents basked in the sun. From the street came the wail of a police siren. I sat in the room and tried to devise a strategy of attack. All I had were theories; I would need further information from allies.

One thing had troubled me; so far as I knew, the Valley police had not been suspicious of Gillete's association with Clauss. I walked to the Santa Monica station and Lars was there. I told him what had been bothering me.

"They had no proof that Gillete had *any* connection with Clauss," he pointed out. "Gillete told them he had fired Tucker because his attorney had told him about some doubtful connections in Tucker's past history. We know the Clauss-Gillete connection, or think we do. They don't."

"That attorney could be Winthrop Loeb, now under investigation by the Feds."

He shrugged. "We cops wouldn't know about that. None of those investigative agencies out of Washington ever confides in us, not even when we're working with 'em. They are real secretive bastards. And what's new by you?"

"Nothing solid. And you?"

"Pissed off. What in hell am I doing here? I'm a cop, not a damned clerk!"

"Have you explained that to your boss?"

"Often. And got nowhere. I've got the feeling that he thinks I'm another Rambo on the street."

I smiled.

"I know what you're thinking," he said. "You may leave now."

"I'm on the way. Lars, if more cops were like you, the streets would be a hell of a lot safer."

"We both know that," he agreed. "And we could be the only ones who do. Be careful out there, buddy."

I nodded, winked at him, and left. To paraphrase an old song, Lars may have been a headache but he had never been a bore.

The Valley police had never uncovered the Clauss-Gillete connection; they had accepted Gillete's story that Tucker had been his only employee. In my phone call to Gillete, he had not denied knowing Clauss. He had confirmed it, I thought, by saying Clauss was not a relative. Gillete was lucky that it wasn't Clauss who had questioned him.

I had no further line of inquiry. I went to the motel for my car. On the way, I had the random thought that Peter Scarlatti also lived in the Pacific Palisades. Was that another line of inquiry? Ronald Reagan had lived in the Pacific Palisades before he moved to Washington, I reminded myself.

I would stick with Clauss. He was still the *who*. Nolan, I felt sure, was a key to the *why*. Prying the truth out of a man as evasive as Joe Nolan would be almost impossible. I needed more ammunition. No prosecuting attorney could get a murder-one conviction without the deadly triplicate: motive, means, and opportunity. The motive was the *why*, means and opportunity the *who*.

Joe Nolan had led me down the garden path and wound up in a jungle he hadn't foreseen. If the connection I suspected proved to be true, it included an attorney under Federal investigation, a known hoodlum, and a crooked ex-cop on the prowl.

The criminal jungle is far more dangerous to one's health than the financial jungle. Bankers and brokers and bookies rarely need to carry lethal weapons.

Nolan was the wimp in that threesome and the one most likely to fold under pressure. He would be my first target. Clauss might outshoot me; I felt confident that I could outlie Joe Nolan. It was time to play the blackmail game.

But first I would need some facts not yet in evidence to become evidential enough, to be a threat strong enough, to frighten the truth out of him.

It was getting close to dinnertime and the kids were no longer in the pool. I hadn't brought my swimming trunks with me, but the desk clerk told me they had sanitized swimming trunks for the guests, at no cost.

I was on my twelfth leisurely lap when Lars appeared at the side of the pool. "Anything new?" he asked.

I nodded and climbed out. I took a huge bath towel from the rack and we sat down on deck chairs.

I told him the strategy I had planned this afternoon and the hope that my broker friend would come up with enough to put the heat on Nolan.

"It sounds good to me," he said. He paused. "But you'll be going it alone, Brock. Slade read me the riot act just before I left. We will keep an open file on Mike. But there will be no more investigation unless some new evidence comes in."

"He's a real pompous ass, that Slade, isn't he?"

He nodded. "But, unfortunately, my boss. I'll be available nights—if I'm home. I'm in the book. Call me if you need me."

"I will."

He got up from his chair and left. If I'm home . . . How often, I wondered, did he spend his nights at home?

I went to the room after dinner and the phone was ringing. It was my broker friend. He had confirmed what I suspected; the connection was complete and Nolan was a part of it. Mike, he told me, had probably been guilty of blackmail. He had learned that it was Gillete who had financed Nolan's office. The rumor was that Nolan was now laundering Gillete's dirty dollars.

"But don't quote me," he said. "My source is no friend of Gillete's. Neither one of us wants to get on his hit list. My source is not squeaky clean himself. He's the man who gave Mike the story on Gillete financing Nolan's office."

I thanked him and hung up before he could start a sales pitch on all the advantages I would get if I moved to Hutton.

I considered phoning Nolan at home, but that would only give him time to concoct another silly scenario. Tomorrow was soon enough. The ammunition would keep until then.

CHAPTER TWENTY

Nolan was alone in his office when I got there. He didn't seem happy to see me. "What brings you here this time?" he asked.

"A few questions. First—is Winthrop Loeb your attorney?"

He studied me for seconds before he nodded. "Why do you ask?"

"Because he is being investigated by the Feds."

He shook his head. "Not anymore. He has been cleared. As I told you last time you were here, they had no case. Next question?"

"Why did you tell me that you didn't know who Arnold Gillete was?"

He took a little longer to answer that one. Finally: "Brock, that is none of your business. I don't know what you are trying to prove about me. But if you have any information about *any* illegal activities of mine, I suggest that you take them to the proper authorities. And now I must get back to work."

"Okay," I said. "I'm not an attorney, but I have always believed that laundering dirty money is an illegal activity." I turned toward the door.

"Wait a minute," he said.

I turned back.

"Sit down."

I did.

"Who told you about Loeb being under investigation?"

"A man I once worked with on a murder investigation, a man who has a long family history on the wrong side of the law."

He stared at me. "Who?"

"You won't get his name from me and neither will the Feds. He wasn't the man who told me about your laundering money. You won't get that name, either. Are we going to do business or do you want me to leave?"

He was obviously discombobulated now. "Business? What do you mean, business?"

"Let's call it a deal. I forget all that I have learned about you. The laundering of money, your connection with Gillete, all of it. In return, you tell me where Emil Clauss is hiding."

"Emil Clauss. Who the hell is he?"

"He works for the other man you claimed you didn't know. He's Gillete's hit man. And I'm sure he is the man who murdered Mike Gregory."

He took a deep breath. "Brock, I'll admit I have lied to you, but so help me God, I've never heard of Emil Clauss."

"Gillete has. You could ask him."

"And wind up on welfare? Be reasonable, man!"

"I'm trying to. Gillete must realize by now that Clauss has to go. He can't afford men like that. He dumped Tim Tucker, when he learned about his roughhouse tactics. He even apologized to me about it. Gillete didn't get rich by working with kooks. He's too smart for that."

He nodded, and stared down at his desk. "He's smart, that's for sure. Maybe he'd listen to me."

"I'm sure he would. I don't give a tinker's damn about your financial manipulations. My sole interest in this whole sordid mess is nailing the man who murdered Mike Gregory."

"That's some deal! Clauss goes to jail and makes his own deal with the DA. So Arnold and I wind up in jail with him. That's worse than welfare."

"Dead men can't testify," I said.

"What are you saying?"

"You know what I'm saying. And I have a cop friend who agrees with me. Both of us would rather see Clauss dead than have him wind up with a minimum sentence and walking the streets again. With me, it's more personal."

"I can guess who your cop friend is," he said. "Lars Hovde."

I smiled at him. "Who is Lars Hovde?"

"You are really a cute one," he said.

"We sure are, aren't we? Deal?"

He sighed and shrugged. "Give me some time on this. Let me think about. You've got me between a rock and a hard place. I'll phone you after I talk with Arnold. He's out of town now, but he'll be home tonight. Are you still at the Beverly Hills Hotel?"

"Nope. I'll phone you."

He nodded.

I left without saying good-bye. His lies had made him rich; the truth could set him free. It was priority time again for Joe Nolan.

Was Gillete, I wondered, really out of town. Or was that another ploy of Nolan's to stall me until he could come up with a battle plan of his own?

Heinie's was the nearest phone. I stopped in there and used his office phone to call Gillete. A woman answered and I asked to speak with him.

173

He was out of town, she told me, but would be home tonight. Did I wish to leave a message?

"Yes. Please tell him to call his broker as soon as he gets home. It is very important."

Nolan hadn't lied—for a change. The man was frightened and had reason to be. That was the way I wanted him to be. But Gillete was made of sterner stuff. He lived in a different world, a world of chicanery and violence. Chicanery was not alien to Nolan's world; the daily papers testified to that. But if push came to shove, it was possible that Gillete would be inclined to favor a man out of his own world, a man of violence. Clauss.

To Gillete's way of thinking it might be Nolan who was expendable, not his stalwart soldier. And when Nolan explained to him that I was the source of incriminating evidence against him, I, too, could make his hit list.

Young Dennis Sadler had opted out, a wise move. He was too young to die. It was my personal feeling that I was also too young to die. Read him how you will, Mike had also been too young to die. And as my father had told me, *nobody* should get away with murder.

It was still well short of noon. I stopped at the station to tell Lars about my dialogue with Nolan. He wasn't at his desk and the desk sergeant didn't know where he was.

Back at the motel, the desk clerk told me a man had been in and asked to see me.

"Did he leave a name?"

He shook his head. He took a deep breath. "I suppose I should have asked him." He paused. "It's possible I did something you might not approve of. To tell you the truth, Mr. Callahan, I

174

didn't like his looks. I hope you won't report this to the manager, but I told the man that you had checked out."

"What did he look like?"

"Disreputable is the closest word I can think of to describe him. He was bald and bulky and had snow-white eyebrows."

"You did the right thing," I told him. "You probably saved my life. I'm sure he's the man the Santa Monica police are looking for right now."

He stared at me. "What if he didn't believe me? Do you think he might come back?"

"I doubt it. He took a big chance showing himself in town. Of course, there's the possibility he might make the same mistake again. I'll call the station and inform them. I'm sure they'll send an officer over."

I phoned the station from my room and asked for Chief Denzler. He assured me that though they were badly understaffed, he would send a man over to sit in the lobby for a limited time.

I thought of suggesting to him that the man they send should not be in uniform. That would alert Clauss. I didn't suggest it; that would be unkind. He was getting enough abuse from the local paper.

How had Clauss learned where I was staying? Certainly not from Nolan. I believed him when he had told me he had never heard of the man. Gillete was out of town. Clauss must have learned it from one of the local hoodlums.

A thin, tall man in gray slacks and a blue jacket was sitting next to the paperback rack in the lobby when I went down for lunch. I had seen him at the Santa Monica station but knew him by his own name, Lou.

He nodded to me and I went over. "Have you had lunch?" I asked him. "You can still see the desk from the lunchroom, and we can watch the street, too."

"Good thinking," he said. "I've already had lunch, but I can use a cup of coffee. I hope you're carrying."

I nodded. "A Galanti."

He smiled. "That should be enough."

At the table I told him I had phoned Lars that morning, but he hadn't been in. He told me Lars had left the station at ten o'clock with two other officers and he didn't know what their mission was. Lars, he said, always came in to the station at the end of his watch. That would be around five o'clock.

"He really hates Clauss, doesn't he?"

"So do I. Lars has more reason to hate him. Clauss used to be a cop."

He nodded. "Crooked cops, they're the worst. They know how we operate and they still have all their informants when they move to the other side of the street."

We moved to the financial world from there and all the chicanery that was now going on there.

"Maybe we should switch priorities," I suggested. "You boys could keep an eye on Wall Street and the Feds could go after the hoodlums."

"The Feds, shit!" he said. "They're not cops, they're politicians. The big money boys don't go to the can often enough. They can afford millionaire lawyers."

He went back to his chair in the lobby. I went out to the pool and sat in the shade of a parasol.

Tonight could be the end of the hunt. But maybe

not. Trusting a pair like Nolan and Gillete to come through was no more than an even bet. And if Clauss learned they were planning to shaft him, I would not be the only member of his revenge list. If the clerk at the desk hadn't lied, Clauss could have eliminated me from his hit file.

At three o'clock I phoned Nolan and asked him when Gillete would be back from his trip.

"Around seven," he said. "I'm going to his house after dinner to tell him about your deal. I'm not sure he'll agree it's a smart move, but I hope he does. He can be stubborn."

"I'll phone there at eight."

"Make it eight-thirty, in case his plane is late. They usually are these days."

"Eight-thirty," I agreed.

What could be a wise move for Nolan might not be a wise move for Gillete. Nolan had a reputation to maintain; Gillete's was not important to him. He knew it was bad. His concern was staying out of jail.

Why, I wondered, *if* Clauss was working for Gillete, had he holed up in that fetid building where Tucker had taken him? Gillete could certainly have afforded and arranged a less odorous hiding place than that.

Too many questions and not enough answers; I thought of all the questions I intended to ask Gillete if he was willing to deal.

A few minutes before five o'clock I phoned the station and Lars was there. I told him about my dialogue with Nolan and what he had promised to do if Gillete was agreeable.

"Jesus!" he said. "What was your leverage? I smell something fishy, Brock."

"What else do we have? We work with what we can get. Maybe we should take a few more officers with us."

"So Slade can get credit for the pinch? Like hell! We'll handle this alone. And if we blow it, who will know? We have nothing to lose, man."

"Nothing but our lives."

"Buddy, if you want to back out, I'll go it alone."

"Did Denzler tell you Clauss came to the hotel this afternoon, looking for me?"

"No. He was gone when I came in. Well, now we know Clauss is still in town. Are you in or out, Brock?"

"In."

"Good." He gave me his address and said, "You can phone Gillete from there."

Cowboy Lars . . . It wasn't the ink Slade would get that had troubled him. It was the thought that Slade and his friends might not share his view of justice for some, but not for *all*, and Clauss would walk the streets again.

I was still a little leery about this mission. Both Gillete and Nolan could claim that it was I who had suggested killing Clauss. There was no record of that. But both Gillete and Nolan could claim that I had suggested it, probably supported by Winthrop Loeb.

It was really a case for the SMPD—but what had they learned? Nothing. And would they back me in court? I doubted it. Clauss could walk.

CHAPTER TWENTY-ONE

I drove to Lars's house a little before eight. It was a small, weather-stained stucco house on a cheap street. There was an SMPD patrol car parked in front of it.

I pointed at it when Lars opened the door. "What gives?" I asked. "Have you decided the Department should be involved?"

He shook his head. "Come in."

The door opened directly into the living room. I will not describe the decor, except that it was obvious that he was a bachelor.

"I drove it home," he explained. "If Nolan guessed that I am going to be with you tonight, Clauss could know it, too. That's just a prop out there. We'll use your car. Smart move, right?"

"Brilliant," I said, and tried not to smile.

"I brought us a couple of bullet-proof vests from the station," he said. "Have you eaten?"

I nodded. "But I could use a cup of coffee."

He went into the kitchen. I sat on a couch next to an end table. When he brought the coffee I related my phone call from Nolan, word for word, as well as I could remember them.

He shook his head. "I can't believe Gillete will buy it."

"He might have to. I told Nolan I had mob connections and I think he bought it. If Gillete does, that could be a plus for us. I have a feeling he wants to move up a level or two."

He shook his head again. "I don't know, Brock. I—"

"It's just a theory," I said, "and maybe a wild one. Let's talk about tonight."

We planned our strategy. At eight-thirty, I phoned Gillete.

"Joe has told me about your deal," he said. "I hope you don't think you conned me with that falsetto phone call."

"I tried to. And then you passed on the information to Clauss. He came to visit me today at the place where I was staying. But I was out. If I hadn't been, I'm sure one of us would be dead by now."

"Mr. Callahan, I had no knowledge of where you were staying. And I have no knowledge of how Clauss got the word that you were out to get him. He did *not* get it from me."

"I'll accept that."

"As for Mike Gregory's murder, he tried to blackmail me." He paused. "For a lousy five grand! He was really on his uppers. I sent Clauss with the money to pay him off. That damned fool took his shotgun with him. And that is when I dumped him. And that is the reason I fired Tucker."

"And who killed Tucker?"

"Let's stay with the subject at hand. What about this man you worked with who has a long family history on the wrong side of the law?"

"Mr. Gillete, I don't think either one of us should talk about that. It could be dangerous to our health. As any cop in this area will tell you, I, too, once worked on the wrong side of the law. That was before I could afford to turn honest."

"And Clauss is all you want?"

"Clauss is all I want."

180

"I hope you have a good lawyer," he said, "or police cooperation. We both know Clauss is a weirdo. But killing him could still put you behind bars."

"That," I assured him, "has been taken care of."

A long silence. Then: "I just got the word fifteen minutes ago. I don't know the street address, but it's a cottage on Anchor Street, a short distance from a bar called The Dungeon. Clauss is shacked up there with a woman named Veronica Lang."

"Thank you," I said, and hung up.

"Well?" Lars asked.

I told him what Gillete had told me.

"I know the woman," he said. "I busted her a couple of times. Let's get these jackets on."

We were about a block from Anchor Street when he said, "Park on The Dungeon lot. There's an alley behind Veronica's house. You stay there to watch the back door. I'll take the front."

I nodded.

As we walked past the front window of The Dungeon, I could see the former flyweight boxer, little Ernie, quaffing a beer at the bar. Maybe it was he who had alerted Gillete, but I doubted it.

There was no light showing in the front window of the cottage; the reflection from a side window showed there was a dim light on in one of the windows near the rear of the house.

Lars stayed out on the walk in front, giving me time to go down the alley to the back of the cottage. At the far end of the alley, two shabby men were rummaging in the trash cans there, illuminated by the streetlight at the far end.

I moved into the small yard and crouched behind a bush. The moon was out, the night was cloudless. The scavengers were arguing now. One of them must have unearthed something the other man wanted.

No sound came from the house. Perhaps it was vacant. Lars should have rung the bell or knocked on the door by now. It was hard to believe that Gillete had conned us. He had too much to lose.

And then I heard Lars shout, "Damn you, Veronica, open the door! I'm not here to bust you."

Less than a minute later, I heard the rasp of the dimly lit side window opening. And the bald head of Emil Clauss emerged.

"Don't do anything foolish, Emil!" I shouted. "You're covered all around."

The head disappeared.

Seconds later, there was the blast of what had to be a shotgun. I ran through the yard to the front of the house.

Lars was lying on the sidewalk below the porch. I didn't see any blood. "That bastard!" he said. "He shot right through the door!"

He rose slowly and rubbed the back of his neck. "Thank God for the jacket. The door slowed enough of the pellets to keep me alive, but not enough to keep me on my feet. Did you see which way he went?"

I shook my head. "But we have a car and he probably doesn't. Let's go!"

We were heading for The Dungeon parking lot when Ernie stopped us short of the place. "I heard the shot," he said. "Are you looking for Clauss?"

We both nodded.

He pointed at The Dungeon. "Don't tell the boys in there that I finked. It's full of Clauss fans.

Me, I've had enough trouble. He's in the storage room at the back of the joint. He ran in there a couple minutes ago."

"Is there a back door to the room?" Lars asked.

Ernie shook his head. "Two windows. But both of them are screened with heavy netting. He should still be in there."

Lars said to me, "You go back to the alley, Brock. I'll handle this end."

The scavengers were now nowhere in sight. There was a large rubbish can in the alley about forty feet this side of The Dungeon. That would afford me all the cover I would need.

A rasping sound was coming from the storage room. Emil must have found some tool in there to loosen the heavy netting. It wasn't likely that Lars would go into that dim room with the light from the bar framing him in an open doorway.

The rasping sound ended. Again, there was the squeaking sound of a window opening. And again the bald head emerged. This time it swiveled to check both ends of the deserted alley. I crouched lower, my stomach rumbling, the Galanti shaky in my hand.

The head disappeared, one leg emerged. I waited until he was out and standing in the alley before I called, "Drop the gun, Emil!"

He didn't. He spun my way, looking for me, bringing the shotgun up. I didn't yell again; he wouldn't have heard me anyway in the sudden blast of his weapon. He missed me, but I didn't miss him. I put two slugs from the Galanti into his chest. He went down, the shotgun clanging as it bounced on the pavement.

I was bending over him when Lars stuck his head through the open window. "Dead?" he said.

"Dead."

"Give me your gun."

"Why?"

"Don't ask dumb questions. Give me the damn gun and take mine. Go back to the car and wait for me. I'll phone the station from here."

I was back in the car when the ambulance and the squad car showed up. I stayed there until they left again a long time later.

When Lars came, he said, "You can take me home now. I'll take the Department car to the station. I'll bring your Galanti to you at the motel after I'm finished reporting at the station."

I handed him his gun. "I'm the one who shot him, Lars."

"We both know that. Do you want to spend a couple months in court down here claiming self-defense?"

"I don't. But maybe I should."

"And get me into more trouble with Slade? He *hates* private eyes. But he loves to see hoodlums die. He's been getting a lot of static about the Department's lack of interest in nailing Mike's killer, mostly from concerned citizen's groups. We took that load off his back."

I said nothing.

"Brock, if he'd come out into the bar, I'd have nailed him and he'd be just as dead. Jesus, man, grow up!"

I turned on the engine and drove out onto the street. We had no further dialogue on the way to his house. I was emotionally bushed.

When I dropped him off, I said, "Keep the damned Galanti. I don't want it."

He grinned at me. "Thanks. I forgot to get you a permit for it. You could be in deep trouble, buddy, if you kept it."

Some bitter words came to mind, but I didn't voice them. I had come down here and done what I had to do. And he had been more help than hindrance. One more killer would not be back on the streets. Why should I feel guilty about that?

It was only a little after ten o'clock and I was only ninety miles from home. I checked out of the motel and headed for San Valdesto.

CHAPTER TWENTY-TWO

For two days I gave a lot of thought to whether I should or should not inform the Feds about the Gillete-Clauss-Nolan connection. I didn't want to get on to Gillete's hit list.

On the third day, that problem was resolved for me. Nolan had lied to me about Loeb no longer being under observation by the Feds. According to the L.A. *Times,* Loeb had been suspected—and smart lawyer that he was, he had turned informant on himself, and on Nolan and Gillete, in exchange for a minimal sentence.

Nolan had cracked, too, under pressure. He was the one who had put the arsenic in Terrible Tim Tucker's whiskey. He was afraid of Tucker, afraid of winding up beaten to death like Barney Luplow —that was one reason. Another was that he'd found out Gillete wanted to get rid of Tucker in order to make himself more acceptable to the mob. Nolan figured poisoning Tucker would put him in solid with Gillete. Not too smart. But what else would you expect from a crook, a liar, and an effing stockbroker?

On the fourth day, Jan came home and all was serene again in the life of Brock Callahan.

CARROLL & GRAF

FINE MYSTERY AND SUSPENSE
TITLES FROM CARROLL & GRAF

☐ Allingham, Margery/MR. CAMPION'S
FARTHING $3.95

☐ Allingham, Margery/MR. CAMPION'S
QUARRY $3.95

☐ Allingham, Margery/NO LOVE LOST $3.95

☐ Allingham, Margery/THE WHITE COTTAGE
MYSTERY $3.50

☐ Ambler, Eric/BACKGROUND TO DANGER $3.95

☐ Ambler, Eric/CAUSE FOR ALARM $3.95

☐ Ambler, Eric/A COFFIN FOR DIMITRIOS $3.95

☐ Ambler, Eric/EPITAPH FOR A SPY $3.95

☐ Ambler, Eric/STATE OF SIEGE $3.95

☐ Ambler, Eric/JOURNEY INTO FEAR $3.95

☐ Ball, John/THE KIWI TARGET $3.95

☐ Bentley, E.C./TRENT'S OWN CASE $3.95

☐ Blake, Nicholas/A TANGLED WEB $3.50

☐ Brand, Christianna/DEATH IN HIGH HEELS $3.95

☐ Brand, Christianna/GREEN FOR DANGER $3.95

☐ Brand, Christianna/FOG OF DOUBT $3.50

☐ Brand, Christianna/TOUR DE FORCE $3.95

☐ Brown, Fredric/THE LENIENT BEAST $3.50

☐ Brown, Fredric/MURDER CAN BE FUN $3.95

☐ Brown, Fredric/THE SCREAMING MIMI $3.50

☐ Browne, Howard/THIN AIR $3.50

☐ Buchan, John/JOHN MACNAB $3.95

☐ Buchan, John/WITCH WOOD $3.95

☐ Burnett, W.R./LITTLE CAESAR $3.50

☐ Butler, Gerald/KISS THE BLOOD OFF MY
HANDS $3.95

☐ Carr, John Dickson/CAPTAIN CUT-THROAT $3.95

☐ Carr, John Dickson/DARK OF THE MOON $3.50

☐ Carr, John Dickson/THE DEMONIACS $3.95

☐ Carr, John Dickson/FIRE, BURN! $3.50

☐ Carr, John Dickson/THE GHOSTS' HIGH
NOON $3.95

☐ Graham, Winston/MARNIE — $3.95
☐ Griffiths, John/THE GOOD SPY — $4.95
☐ Hornung, E.W./THE AMATEUR CRACKSMAN — $3.95
☐ Hughes, Dorothy B./THE EXPENDABLE MAN — $3.50
☐ Hughes, Dorothy B./THE FALLEN SPARROW — $3.50
☐ Hughes, Dorothy B./IN A LONELY PLACE — $3.50
☐ Hughes, Dorothy B./RIDE THE PINK HORSE — $3.95
☐ Kitchin, C. H. B./DEATH OF HIS UNCLE — $3.95
☐ Kitchin, C. H. B./DEATH OF MY AUNT — $3.50
☐ MacDonald, John D./TWO — $2.50
☐ MacDonald, Philip/THE RASP — $3.50
☐ Mason, A.E.W./AT THE VILLA ROSE — $3.50
☐ Mason, A.E.W./THE HOUSE OF THE ARROW — $3.50
☐ McShane, Mark/SEANCE ON A WET AFTERNOON — $3.95
☐ Muller & Pronzini/BEYOND THE GRAVE — $3.95
☐ Pentecost, Hugh/THE CANNIBAL WHO OVERATE — $3.95
☐ Priestley, J.B./SALT IS LEAVING — $3.95
☐ Pronzini & Greenberg/THE MAMMOTH BOOK OF PRIVATE EYE STORIES — $8.95
☐ Queen, Ellery/THE FINISHING STROKE — $3.95
☐ Rogers, Joel T./THE RED RIGHT HAND — $3.50
☐ 'Sapper'/BULLDOG DRUMMOND — $3.50
☐ Stevens, Shane/BY REASON OF INSANITY — $5.95
☐ Symons, Julian/BOGUE'S FORTUNE — $3.95
☐ Symons, Julian/THE BROKEN PENNY — $3.95
☐ Wainwright, John/ALL ON A SUMMER'S DAY — $3.50
☐ Wallace, Edgar/THE FOUR JUST MEN — $2.95

☐ Waugh, Hillary/A DEATH IN A TOWN $3.95
☐ Waugh, Hillary/LAST SEEN WEARING $3.95
☐ Waugh, Hillary/SLEEP LONG, MY LOVE $3.95
☐ Westlake, Donald E./THE MERCENARIES $3.95
☐ Willeford, Charles/THE WOMAN CHASER $3.95
☐ Wilson, Colin/A CRIMINAL HISTORY OF
   MANKIND $13.95